A BALLET OF LEPERS

BY LEONARD COHEN

POETRY

Let Us Compare Mythologies (1956)
The Spice-Box of Earth (1961)
Flowers for Hitler (1964)
Parasites of Heaven (1966)
Selected Poems: 1956-1968 (1968)
The Energy of Slaves (1972)
Death of a Lady's Man (1978)
Book of Mercy (1984)
Stranger Music: Selected Poems and Songs (1993)
Book of Longing (2006)
The Flame (2018)

FICTION

The Favourite Game (1963)
Beautiful Losers (1966)

LEONARD COHEN

EDITED BY

ALEXANDRA PLESHOYANO

A BALLET OF LEPERS

A NOVEL AND STORIES

McClelland & Stewart

Published in the United States of America by Grove Atlantic
and in Great Britain by Canongate Books Ltd.

Library and Archives Canada Cataloguing in Publication
Title: A ballet of lepers : a novel and stories / Leonard Cohen.
Other titles: Works. Selections (McClelland & Stewart)
Names: Cohen, Leonard, 1934-2016, author.
Identifiers: Canadiana (print) 2022019047X | Canadiana (ebook)
20220190496 | ISBN 9780771018145 (hardcover) |
ISBN 9780771018176 (EPUB)
Classification: LCC PS8505.O22 A6 2022 | DDC C813/.54—dc23

Book design by Kelly Hill
Jacket art courtesy of the Leonard Cohen Family Trust
Typeset in Goudy by M&S, Toronto
Printed in the United States of America

McClelland & Stewart,
a division of Penguin Random House Canada Limited,
a Penguin Random House Company
www.penguinrandomhouse.ca

1 2 3 4 5   26 25 24 23 22

Penguin
Random House
McCLELLAND & STEWART

CONTENTS

Novel

Short Stories

A BALLET OF LEPERS

A NOVEL

Do I contradict myself?

— WALT WHITMAN

I

My grandfather came to live with me. There was nowhere else for
him to go. What had happened to all his children? Death, decay,
exile—I hardly know. My own parents died of pain. But I must
not be too gloomy, at the beginning, or you will leave me and
that, I suppose, is what I dread most. Who would begin a story
if he knew it were to end with a climbing chariot or a cross? The
landlady discovered an extra bed somewhere and put it in my
room. She raised the rent from nine to eleven dollars. After all,
she said, it's another person using the bathroom. She was right.
The poor old man had a weak bladder and he also had to spit
frequently. I was surprised at how well he spoke English. I do not
remember my parents speaking so well. When they came over,
they promised each other that they would never speak another
word of their mother tongue. "We begin again, all again," my
father said on many occasions. I remember their slow painful
speech as they tried to convey the smallest items to each other.
I do not think they ever broke their promise, even in the privacy

of their beds. As I grow older, I realize how monumental was their individual isolation. They even refused to develop a private vocabulary of facial expressions. When my mother tried to use her beautiful eyes and hands to describe something, my father said, "No, no, begin again, English." No subtleties, no intimacies, no secrets—they died, I'm sure, of loneliness. I never heard much about my grandfather. In fact, I thought he had died. I understand my parents used to send him a little money each month but I'm not positive. Nothing was very clear in our house and besides they didn't like to involve me in anything that had to do with the past.

Last week, it was towards the end of the week, I received a telephone call. The door of my room was closed, of course, and I was sitting in the room's only chair looking out at Stanley Street. The thickening night was beginning to hide the ugliness of the street. Even the stream of huge, absurd automobiles was dimming into a movement of beauty and I could not see the faces of the drivers as they went by. Down the hall, the telephone rang. I concentrated on a couple beneath my window. My window was closed, or rather, jammed so that I could not open it and I could not hear what they were saying to each other. It was obviously an argument. She leaned against one of the parked cars, hands on hips, immovable. He stood before her, slightly off balance, raising and lowering his open hands with such regularity, he appeared to be juggling invisible oranges. His movement began to irritate me and exactly at that moment, when I became aware of the irritation, the girl seized both of his hands in hers and flung them down. I suppose she shouted at him as I would have liked to do, "And stop waving your goddamn hands at me." I was deep in this delicious observation when I heard footsteps down the hall and recognized my landlady's heavy hand in the knock at the door. I became furious. There are not many privileges attendant to living in a Stanley Street rooming house, but I've always tried to preserve my privacy wherever I've gone. I have asked for nothing but to be left alone when I needed solitude. No, please do not turn away, I do not mean you. I had made it clear to my landlady that I never wanted to be disturbed in the evening. First of all, because I need my privacy as I've just mentioned, and second because I've always been terrified at being interrupted when I was making love to Marylin. With her knocking I became furious because by it she removed me from the drama of the street and because she had invaded my room.

Even though I can tell you these reasons, and I hope that I'm not being too tedious, I have never fully understood my anger. In fact, sometimes I am frightened by it. It is more of a hate than an anger. On such occasion, as I am describing, it overwhelms me, possesses me, takes me right out of myself. Or maybe I should say right into myself because, as I've said, on these occasions I feel myself stripped of flesh and organs and the truer heart of hate and violence is exposed. Now, I know this might not be very interesting, but I must tell you about myself. I mean what are we here for if I don't do that? When she knocked, and this sudden hate for her consumed me, I wanted to shout at her, anything, a rebuke, an obscenity, anything to express the power of my feelings, but I tightened my body, squeezed my eyes shut, and asked her hoarsely what she wanted.

"Telephone, sorry to disturb you, long distance, New York, America," she explained. "I thought that you'd want to speak."

I was immediately relieved. As swiftly as hatred had consumed me, it was dispersed by her explanation. For a few moments, I indulged myself in the feeling of relief. I observed my body relax, my eyes reopened and focused on the quarrelling couple. They were standing in the same position but now his hands were in his pockets. My heart changed from timpani back to slow tom-tom. Again, the landlady reminded me of the telephone. I thanked her and settled back in my chair. I have long known that we are blind in the midst of an act. All wisdom is in anticipation. I speculated as to whom the call was from and what its nature would be. I pictured myself holding the receiver, felt the shape of black plastic in my hand, imagined the odor of my landlady on it. I heard the distant voice, accepted the message, digested it. When I had exhausted all the pictures in my mind, I stood up and walked to the door. I was already weary of the event. It was as though it had already happened. Now, there was only a token time I must spend with the black instrument to pay for my delightful speculation. I resented placing the hard circle against my ear. I would hear only one voice and before I had heard and dissected a chorus. I would receive only one message and before I had received news, verdicts, laws, prohibitions, and secrets. I spoke my name into the perforated mouthpiece.

"Ah," said a voice, heavy with foreign intonation, "we are so happy to have found you at last."

"Found me?"

"Yes, we knew he had grandson, a grandson in Montreal. Your father's name was Frederik?"

"Yes, that was his name."

"We can't keep him any longer. We surely can't. If we had the money, but we don't, and besides we're not even the family. When your father sent the money, it was different. We like him, I tell you we like him, he is a very nice old man. But now, it is too hard for my wife, she can't anymore take care of him."

"Just a moment. You mean to say that my grandfather is living with you now?"

"Yes, yes, I tell you. Even after the money stopped, we kept him. We like him but now it's too hard. He is sick, he must be watched."

"Yes, yes, of course. How did you know about me?"

"The old man, he told us he had someone in Montreal. He remembered your name, he had it written down somewhere, it was in a letter your father must have sent, we saw it with your name on it. Frederik was your father, yes? We looked up your number in the Montreal phone book in a hotel."

"Yes, yes, extraordinary, after all this time."

"We would have kept him even without the money, but she is tired and sick herself, my wife. Listen, we cannot speak longer, the long-distance costs too much. He knows we can't keep him any longer and he wants to go to you, the old man. He wants to be among his family. You will take him?"

"I have very little myself, just a room, but of course he must come here."

"Good, good, you are a good grandson. We have bought already the train ticket. We can't go with him. We'll put him on the train, and you will meet him in Montreal. It says here the train will arrive eleven o'clock Wednesday night. You will meet him, he will be very happy. Do you understand everything?"

"Yes, eleven o'clock Wednesday night. Will I be able to recognize him?"

"An old man, an old man. He often says you look just like him."

"Good. I will be there, and I want to thank you for all that you've done, you and your wife, and I hope that she feels better."

But before I had finished my last sentence, he had hung down. Immediately, I discussed the situation with my landlady who had been listening to the conversation anyway; the new bed and the new rent were decided upon. I returned to my room and sat before my window. I certainly had not expected this. So, the unexpected does happen occasionally. Slowly, I felt the return of a deep family love, a bond joining the generations one to another. I was looking forward to meeting my grandfather, to sharing my room and food with him, he of my own blood and flesh, he of my own line. What things I would learn, what strength the two of us would have through each other. We belonged together. What was he doing spending his last days with strangers? A pleasant feeling spread over my body. An old love had returned, carrying me back to my own, spilling over the whole street, mixing with the descending night and rendering it fragrant. And as if to confirm my feelings, the couple beneath my window, I could barely see them now, they had ceased their quarrel and were embraced. A man approached them, and they moved away. They were leaning against his car. I stood up and went to my bed. I stood before it and imagined myself lying in it. I lay down and closed my eyes, mixing the colors in a world of love, forming the body of Marylin out of the shadows, waiting with a new patience for her arrival. Where had the embracing couple wandered? Where had he driven to, the man who owned the car? Four hundred miles away, they must be packing the battered valise of an old man. I heard her steps on the outside stairs.

II

"How ardent you are," Marylin said. "Tonight, you are my ardent lover. Tonight, we are gentry and animals, birds and lizards, stone and water, slime and marble. Tonight, we are glorious and degraded, knighted and crushed, beautiful and disgusting. Our mouths are glistening with each other's wetness. Sweat is perfume, groans are gold, gasps are bells, shudders are silver. I wouldn't have traded this for the ravages of the loveliest swan. This is why I must have come to you in the first place. This is why I must have left the others, the hundreds who try and snag my ankle with crippled hands as I speed to you."

In the darkness, I caressed her as she spoke, delighted by her poetry, indulged in power and praise, her body submissive, her voice exalted and adoring for evermore, for evermore.

"For evermore," I said aloud.

This is the kind of romantic game we played when we were at our best. At our worst, it was no game at all but vicious combat. She eased herself out of my arm's clasp and stood up on the bed.

I thought of marble thighs and the knees of stone colossus. She stretched out her arms, shoulder high.

"Christ of the Andes," she proclaimed.

"The Andes themselves," I insisted.

I kneeled below her, nuzzling in her delta.

"Heal me, heal me," I said, with mock supplication.

"Heal me yourself," she cried, laughing and collapsing over me, her face finally resting on my belly.

Later, when we were quiet, I said solemnly, "Woman, thou art loosed from thine infirmity."

She swung her legs onto the floor and danced over to the table and lit the candle in my tin Mexican candelabra. Holding the light above her head, like a religious symbol, she danced back to the bedside and took my hand.

"Come with me, my beast, my swain, my ravager," she chanted. "The mirror, eunuchs, the mirror."

We stood before the mirror and she swept the light of the candle over us like a soft luminous paintbrush.

"Who shall say we are not beautiful?" she challenged.

"Indeed," I responded, "who shall say?"

For a minute or two, we inspected our thirty-five-year-old bodies. And truly at that moment our flesh, flesh which we all know dies swiftly and unlovely, was beautiful. She placed the candelabra on a table beside us and, still watching our images in the glass, we carefully embraced.

"Life has not passed us by after all," she said.

I hoped that she would not begin to reflect, a process by which she usually saddened both of us. I sat in the chair before the window and she on my lap.

"We are lovers," she began, as if she were stating the axioms before attempting a geometry proposition.

"If one of those people on the street now would look up, someone with very good eyes, he would see a naked woman held by a naked man," she continued. "That person would become immediately aroused, wouldn't he, the way we become aroused when we read a provoking sexual description in a novel."

I winced at the word *sexual*. There is no word more inappropriate when two are locked in a sexual embrace.

"And that is the way," she went on, "that is the way most lovers try to regard each other even after they have been intimate for some time."

Intimate, that was another of those words.

"It is a great mistake," she said. "The thrill of the forbidden, the thrill of the naughty is quickly expended, and lovers are soon bored with each other, their sexual identities become more and more vague until they are lost altogether."

"What is the alternative?" I inquired through a growing anger.

"It is to make that which is permitted thrilling," she said. "The lover must totally familiarize himself with his beloved. He must know her every movement, the motion of her buttocks when she walks, the direction of every tiny earthquake when she heaves her chest, the way her thighs spread like lava when she sits down, he must know the sudden coil her stomach makes just before the brink of climax, each orchard of hair, blonde and black, the path of pores on her nose, the charts of vessels in her eyes, the special wound color of lips. He must know her so completely, so thoroughly, that she becomes in effect his own creation. He has molded the shape of her limbs, he has distilled the smell she generated. This is the only successful kind of sexual love, the love of the creator for his creation, in other words, the love of the creator for himself. This love can change, it can evolve and overcome agony and ecstasy, betrayal cannot infect its blind loyalty, it can alter but never diminish."

As she spoke these words to me, her voice became more and more charged with emotion. She delivered the last few sentences with a kind of ecstatic frenzy. I had ceased to caress her, her repeated use of clinical terms having nearly sickened me. She noticed a withdrawal.

"What is the matter?" she asked. "Why have you stopped holding me?"

"Why must you always do this?" I began, my voice hoarse and throat constricted with anger. "Why must you always do this? I have just made love to you. We gave each other love and praise. Couldn't you just sit with me and enjoy the aftermath of pleasure and the peace which follows expression? Did you have to begin the operation, the autopsy? *Sexual, intimate*—I want you to lie softly in my arms. *Distill, generate*—is this a brewery? I don't want to memorize every landscape, I want to be startled every once in a while by a new shiver. I want to be startled every once in a while by a moan which is more profound than the rest. Where are you going?"

She stood before me. The candlelight sketched her mouth, hardened with anger.

"'A new shiver, a moan more profound than the rest,'" she mocked. "O Christ, but you're a fool, a fool like the dozen other men who I've slept with. Yes, a dozen men like you who wanted to make love in the dark, in silence, eyes bound, ears stuffed, flesh sheathed. Men who tired of me and I of them. And you fly off into one of your stupid intolerably frequent rages because I want something different for us. You don't know the difference between creation and masturbation. And there is a difference, you know. You didn't understand a thing I said."

"Double talk," I shouted, not in anger now but desperation. "Double talk, double talk, touble dalk." O God, I spluttered.

"We don't know what we're saying," she said, the anger gone.

"Why couldn't you just lie in my arms?"

"You're hopeless," she said. "Where are my things?"

I watched her dress, my mind a blank, no, not a blank but numb. And as she dressed, as she covered her soft flesh, one area after the other, the numbness grew, bathed my throat like a wind of ether, dissolved the cover of my skin until I was blurred in the air of the room, part of the inanimate room. She walked toward the door. I anticipated the neat noise of the terrible latch. She paused, her hand on the knob.

"Stay," I whispered.

She ran towards me and embraced me. The texture of her clothes was strange against my skin. She wet my cheek and neck with her tears.

She too spoke a whisper, "We haven't the time to hurt each other, we're not children, we're growing old, who cares for us in the street below, no driver will dim his lights for us. I'm frightened we've rejected everything, we're not part of anything. We met, the two of us, on the outside of the city."

"Don't cry, don't cry, don't cry." I stroked her hair. "Forgive me, forgive me, you're beautiful, you're a beautiful woman."

"We can't tire of each other," she pleaded, "we can't, we can't. I'm so tired, I don't want any more affairs, I don't want to know anyone else, I only want to know you."

During her grief, I took possession of myself again. I have noted many times during my life, sadly, that only when faced with extremes of emotion in others can I confirm my own stability. Her grief restored me, made me manly and compassionate. I led her to the bed. She was sobbing, the hiccup sob of a small girl.

"I'm so old, God, I'm so old."

She lay in my uncovered arms.

"You are beautiful," I lied compassionately. "You will always be beautiful."

Soon, she fell asleep in my arms, her body against mine somehow heavier than it had ever been. It seemed as though she were leaded and swollen with grief. I dreamed of a huge cloak flung onto my shoulders from a weeping man in a flying cart. In the morning, she had left as usual before I awakened.

III

I must confess that I was not at all pleased with Marylin's exhibition that night. She seemed intent on destroying our simple relationship with clinical analysis and absurd declarations of futility. Why did she have to bring spoken sorrow into the affair? There was sorrow enough without enunciation, sorrow enough without dissection. She knew very well that sometime, sooner or later, we would have to part; weariness, boredom, they would part us. What was the use of pretending or making up silly theories about a love based on complete familiarity? Why should we be any different from the rest? They part who exchange promises of eternity as surely as they who have the honesty to remain silent. Last year's beloveds are the same as this year's, it is only the lovers who have changed. Love is constant, only the lovers change. I sometimes picture the whole thing as a great game of musical chairs. When the music stops, a few, very few unfortunate ones, cannot continue in the game; the rest find a place to sit before the music starts again. In the scramble, of course, there are bruised knees and hearts, even an assault or a murder, and literature is composed of these casualties but usually one chair is as good as another. I do not say this is not sad. Everyone knows it is sad, still we do not have to advertise the sadness. It is like the sadness at the end of a pleasant meal with good friends in a land of prosperity or the embrace of brothers in a city torn by civil war. Marylin is right, we did meet outside the city but, in some way, everyone is outside the city. Where is the city anyway? It no longer has walls. Never before have the rich and poor shared so many of the same things or the diseased and the whole lived so close together. Over a thousand years ago, a Chinese poet wrote, "The World cheats those who hold no rank." It is true I hold no rank. I am on my third clerical job in three months and Marylin, a woman with five thousand good books behind her, is only a salesgirl at Eaton's. So what? How different is any function today? Rank holder or not, I think that most people lead an underground existence, except that the roof of the crypt has been blown off and everything is exposed and yet exposure changes nothing. And Marylin should have known that in such a wall-less city, where the ill and well go hand in hand, she should put away her leper's bell and dance with everyone who asks. These were my thoughts as I waited in the hot and crowded railroad station for the train, which was bearing my grandfather to me.

IV

I stood my ground as the crowd from the train platform emerged through the gates into the station. I had not been in such a place for some time and was surprised at the happiness around me. I had always remembered stations as depressing places but here were hundreds of men and women and children greeting each other, hugging, exchanging gifts, every face full of promise. I looked for my grandfather, very aware now of my impatience, wanting to greet and embrace him, wanting to participate in this lovely spectacle of human joy. Tomorrow, the bickering and dissatisfaction could resume but tonight every man was being welcomed in his home. Where was he, where was my grandfather? The crowd was beginning to thin, families and luggage spinning out the door into the street. I looked for an old man who would be looking for me. Perhaps something had happened to him: an old man, a long train ride, it was very possible. They should have travelled with him, I thought bitterly; imagine letting an old man come all this way alone. I imagined him in the hot coach, sprawled against the yellow straw seats, swallowing the foul air in painful gasps.

I saw a small knot of people at another gate and I went to investigate. I saw my grandfather in the middle of the group and recognized him immediately. He had my father's great chin and his large clouded eyes. His face was dug with deep, incredible wrinkles, as if his face had been held against a white-hot grill. At the bridge his nose began straight but it ended in a misshapen bulb, the pores large and rivered with blue veins. His suit was too big for him, the jacket hung like a cape from his broad shoulders, and he wore an oversized tarnished chain on his vest. With both hands he leaned on a carved cane. He was spitting at a policeman who held his arm.

"You can't spit here," the policeman said, "it's against the law, there's a sign in two languages, '*Défense de cracher*. No Spitting, forty dollar fine.'"

It was evident my grandfather didn't understand a word the policeman said. I think that all he understood was that the policeman was trying to prohibit him from spitting, something he found intolerable, and so he had commenced to cover the shoes of the officer with saliva. The small crowd, highly amused, was on my grandfather's side.

"Drown him," one said.

"Pick on someone your own size," said another.

"Look behind you," said another, "someone's trying to steal the train."

The policeman increased his grip on the old man's arm.

"You're going to come with me," he said, ignoring the jibes.

"Crown him, pop," one said.

"And in this corner, wearing blue trunks and a brass badge."

"What, what?" my grandfather said to everything.

I fought through the crowd which seemed to be closing in on this humorous altercation.

"Officer," I said, "this is my grandfather."

"What, what?" said my grandfather.

"I am your grandson," I told him, slowly thumping my index finger against my chest.

"What, what?"

He stepped toward me, the policeman having released his arm and with his face close to mine he examined me carefully.

"You?" he asked.

"Yes, yes," I replied a little impatiently, "I'm your grandson."

"He's very old," I said to the policeman.

"Look at my shoes," the policeman said, "if he's in your charge you're going to have to come along too. There's a law against spitting, see that sign and look at my shoes."

"Tut, tut," said someone, "the mayor will give you another pair."

"We have to buy our own shoes and they cost money," the policeman said righteously.

My grandfather embraced me. There were tears in his eyes. He stepped back, shaking his head up and down in an affirmative sign. He waved his hand at me, appealing to the crowd. Even the policeman seemed touched by this scene of recognition.

"Merry Christmas, God bless us, every one," said a young man who looked like a college student.

Then my grandfather stepped up to the policeman and with a great *pah*, spit into his face. The old man doubled up with laughter. A good many in the crowd chuckled. I was electrified.

What followed happened so quickly that it stunned everyone. For a second, the policeman did not move, his face white with rage. Then he seized my grandfather by the lapels and shook him violently up and down shouting something I could not make out. My grandfather did not stop laughing, he was enjoying himself immensely and began jumping up and down following the policeman's motions. I was about to intervene in this absurd dance when suddenly my grandfather jumped a step backward and holding his cane in both hands brought it down with a loud crack on the temple of the policeman. Even in the turmoil of the moment, I remember noting the agility and grace with which my grandfather accomplished his assault. He was beside himself with glee as the policeman collapsed on the marble floor, a dangerous wound in his forehead. He danced around the body, waving his cane like a banner, spitting as he danced on the suffering, speechless man. The spectators were numbed by this bizarre display of violence. I could see that their sympathies were instantly transferred to the stricken man and did not know what to expect from them. Violence is contagious, and they had been exposed to a strong dose. Did I imagine their faces beginning to twist into expressions of fury? I grabbed my grandfather's hand and dived into the crowd, the people parting before us without a protest as we fled.

"For Christ's sake, somebody help him," I heard a voice shout as we lurched through the revolving doors into the street.

The night hid us. The lights were not working on one side of the street and we plunged into the darkness, my grandfather holding tightly on to my hand and chuckling as he ran. I looked back and there seemed to be no unusual disturbance under the station marquee, so we slowed down to a walk. I tried to let go of his hand, but he insisted on holding on to me. He stopped in an alleyway, a few feet from a restaurant entrance, and walked into the shadows. I heard him urinate. I stood there uneasily, waiting for him, inspecting my watch as if I were expecting someone who was late. I wondered if the people passing could hear him. Finally, he emerged and took my hand again. He breathed heavily as we walked up the street to my room, for the first time, showing effects of the train ride and the ordeal in the station. He clung his cane against a lamppost that we passed and laughed and did a little dance step. I laughed too, somehow very proud of the old man.

Slowly, we climbed the stairs to my rooming house, he could only manage one step at a time. He still held my hand, releasing it only once during the climb to pat my shoulder and mutter something which sounded like "Good boy." When we reached the balcony, he leaned over the railing and spit into the street, winking at me as he did so. When we got into my room, he fell immediately on my own bed and in a few seconds was asleep, his shoes and clothes unremoved.

I stood before the window, the old man snoring behind me, trying to chart my own feelings about the events of the evening. I was happy to be his grandson, an emotion I could not fully understand. Provoked or not, he had acted in an extremely brutal manner in the train station. He had danced over the body of a man he had wounded. He had urinated in an alley a few feet from public traffic, an act which usually would disgust me. But now, I was not disgusted. Actually, I laughed with a kind of admiration. The bond of blood seemed more important to me than anything. The bond of family, the bond of love. I lay down in the bed that had been prepared for him. A car making a U-turn in the street cast, for a moment, two white beams into my dark room, the driver gunned his motor and the light disappeared. I leaned over and took hold of my grandfather's hand. He woke up with a grunt.

"Grandfather, Grampa," I began, my voice making its own words, my mind listening with interest and approval, "I'm sorry to wake you up, I want to welcome you, I didn't have a chance before, I want to tell you how happy I am to have you live with me."

"What, what?" he said, sitting up.

"Glad you are here," I said slowly emphasizing each word. "I am glad that you have come to live with me. I don't have very much but we will share everything."

"Sleep," he said, pointing outside at the night.

"Yes," I agreed, patting his hand, "tomorrow we will try and talk. This has been a long night."

"What, what?" he said, withdrawing his hand abruptly.

"Sleep."

"Ah," he said, kicking off his shoes.

"Goodnight," I said, and "goodnight" was the silent echo of the room filled with my possessions, "goodnight" answered the street canyoned with the houses and stores.

I knew by heart, "goodnight" was the moan of the stricken policeman in his violent sleep. Negro floor washers would mop the blood from the marble. The trains would go on back and forth across the wheat-gold back of Canada, plunging down on steel ladders into America. Marylin would love me for a season. Someone would nurse and mend a torn forehead. Pausing in the entrance of sleep, I thought I felt my own forehead bleeding, but it was only sweat. My grandfather beside me, for some reason I did not wish to explore, gauging my breathing to his, I was finally part of the pulsing world of love.

V

I do not know if I will be able to make believable the rest of the story which I must tell you. When I look back on that period of my life, which I am obliged to describe, I see that I was infected by a kind of madness, the kind of madness that infects divided houses and nations during war. I do not really want to understand it because by understanding it, I will have to relive it, and that I could not bear. I desire only your love by the telling.

My grandfather and I, we both awakened early the next morning. He sat up on the bed and nodded to me. With his palms he smoothed down his yellow-white hair. We had both slept with our clothes on and the room was stuffy. I had forgotten to open the good window. He got up from the bed and walked to the window which was jammed. In the morning light, I saw him more clearly. He looked considerably older now and more fragile as he struggled with the window. I remarked to myself how much he looked like my father, the large round skull, the heavy-hanging jaw, and even the shoulders, though now in ruin, suggesting that they had once been strong and straight.

"The window is stuck, Grampa," I told him.

He paid no attention but continued to struggle with it. Then he seized a small bronze figure of Byron, which I kept on the windowsill, and smashed the glass.

"No," I protested, rushing to his side, "you can't do that."

But it was done. He removed the pieces of glass that remained in the frame and threw them into the street. I noted, with relief, that the street was empty. He opened his jacket and vest and flapped them in the breeze which the broken window now afforded. I also undid my tie and enjoyed the new coolness. This was his second act of violence in the few hours I had known him. And this one, like the first, seemed to have its own logic. A policeman had humiliated him, so he had retaliated. An immoveable window had resisted him, so he smashed it. I was not at all startled. *The landlady will be disturbed*, I thought vaguely. He leaned out the window and spit on the sidewalk, his head and shoulders pushed through the empty frame, a dribbling gargoyle above the street. I made us some breakfast on the burner. He ate very slowly, chewing with great difficulty, cutting the food into absurdly small pieces, lifting each piece to his mouth on the fork like a slow derrick. After breakfast, he looked exhausted and went back to lie on the bed. Fumbling in his jacket pocket, he produced a baggage ticket and waved it at me. I told him I would try and pick his valise up during my lunch hour, but he didn't hear me; he had fallen asleep. I left the room quietly like a mother leaves the room of a sick sleeping child. The landlady was waiting for me in the hall.

"What was the noise?" she inquired. "Did you break the window?"

"The one that didn't work, we broke it, my grandfather and I, trying to open it. I'll take care of getting it fixed, don't worry. I wonder if you'd keep an eye on him while I'm at work, you know, show him around if he wants to know where anything is?"

"Of course," she said, her face inquisitive. "I will take good care of him." She tiptoed away.

During the coffee break, the young man who works with me on the books observed my wrinkled suit.

"You don't mind me saying this," he said softly, "I mean, you're older than me and all that, but I don't think Mr. Rand likes the clothes you're wearing."

"Well, that is serious," I said, "we mustn't offend Mr. Rand."

"No," he said earnestly, "we mustn't. Last night he was going my way and he gave me a lift home. He said that one thing he noticed about a man was the suit he wore. 'Tells you a great deal,' he said. 'Look at that fellow who works with you,' he said, 'you can see where he's going. He'll be a book-keeper all his life. Who's going to promote him when he turns up every day looking like he slept in his clothes?'"

"I do," I said.

"Do what?" he asked.

"Sleep in my clothes. I always sleep in my clothes. It saves me time in the morning. It's an extra ten minutes sleep."

"Well, I'm just passing on to you what he said to me. I guess you're old enough to know what you're doing. How do you like this suit? I drove down to Plattsburg to get it. See, it's got three buttons, a vent in back, and almost no shoulders. That's what they wear in America. It's called the Madison Avenue Look, that's a street in New York City, well I guess you know that."

"Very attractive. I suppose it was expensive?"

"Nearly a whole week's salary. I'm going to have to cut down on my vacation. But I look at it like an investment. It's bound to attract attention, the right kind I mean."

"Did you notice Mr. Rand's suit this morning?"

"Why, yes, it was a brown one, I think," he said, finding the question irrelevant.

"And how many buttons did it have? That's right, it had two buttons, only two buttons. Two buttons seem to be enough for Mr. Rand. And of course, you noticed that his shoulders were padded, considerably padded. Personally, I think he regrets his physique."

"What are you trying to say?"

"Mr. Rand doesn't drive down to America to buy his clothes. Mr. Rand has never heard of Madison Avenue. Mr. Rand shops at Eaton's and always keeps an eye out for a bargain."

"You mean you think he might not like the idea of so fashionable a suit?"

"It is a general rule of the hierarchy that the slave should not go better robed than the master."

"You know, you may have something there. I never thought of that."

When he returned to his desk, I noticed that he had removed his jacket.

"Thanks," he said to me later, "I don't think he noticed, do you?"

"I think you got by this time," I said.

"Do you know," I said to him as we were leaving for lunch, "do you know that my grandfather urinates on the street?"

"What are you talking about?" he said. "What a thing to tell me."

"My grandfather, I'll bet you didn't even know I had one, not only does he urinate on the street, but he also spits indiscriminately, smashes windows, and assaults policemen."

I was speaking loudly.

"You'd better keep your voice down," he said, as we walked to the elevator, "that's Mr. Rand behind us now."

"What was that you said about Mr. Rand?" I asked in a loud stage whisper. "You say you don't think he has any taste. Now, I don't think that's quite fair. I've always known Mr. Rand to be very tasteful."

"For God's sake," he whispered desperately, "please keep quiet. What are you trying to do?"

The three of us entered the elevator together.

"I hope all that trouble with your grandfather is over," I said to the young man.

"What was the trouble, son?" Mr. Rand inquired benevolently.

The young man stammered, his face positively filled with terror.

"The old gentleman," I intervened, "I really shouldn't have brought it up, he, well he exposes himself on the street."

"Ah," said Mr. Rand, "poor old gentleman." He patted the young man's shoulder. "We all have our responsibilities, don't we?"

"Yes, sir," the young man managed.

When we stepped out of the elevator, I said, "I hope you won't be chilly without your jacket."

He looked at me as if he were about to cry.

"Yes," Mr. Rand said, duplicating the paternalism in my voice, "it's still pretty chilly outside and remember what I said to you yesterday about appearance," and he cast a look in my direction.

When Mr. Rand was gone the boy was almost sobbing.

"Why did you do that to me, what were you trying to do? What kind of a person do you think Mr. Rand will think I am? Grandfather showing himself on the street, sloppy appearance. You can wonder what he thinks of me now. What have you got against me?"

"I really don't know," I told him truthfully. "You're stupid and ugly and frightened but that never made any difference before. No, I really don't know. As a matter of fact, I have nothing against you at all. I wish you every success. Flourish by all means!"

"You can't talk to me that way. You've got the same job as I got. What are you anyway? You must be forty and look at the job you got."

"Now you are being cruel," I smiled gently.

"Oh, I'm being cruel after what you did to me in front of Mr. Rand. Look at you and your dirty suit, you're lucky I don't slug you."

I want to record everything just as it happened, my feelings especially. The young man had introduced the notion of violence into the conversation. Suddenly, the whole absurd episode in which I was participating became clear. The young man had intruded in my life, intruded by working beside me, intruded by speaking with me, by observing my clothes, by discussing me with Rand, by involving me in his sickening opportunism. Of course, it was not his fault; it was circumstances. But one does not punish the wind for driving the locusts against your home. One burns the locusts. *Punish, violence,* the two words played like mating animals in my brain. I saw my grandfather, not in ruin now but a shining figure, spitting contempt against our concrete tombs, bravely assaulting blind authority, smashing the permanently clouded windows that close out the fragrance. Violence: the powerful, spontaneous act, cutting, eliminating, punishing, teaching. I seized him by his shoulders and backed him against the wall of the building in which we worked. I frightened him by my sudden gesture.

"Look carefully," I said slowly and viciously.

On the street the passersby paid us no attention at all.

"Look at me, look carefully at me. See my fingernails are dirty, my teeth are yellow, look at my suit, it's old and dirty and not pressed. Do you know what all this means? It means I have nothing to lose. It means I could break your neck against this wall and be tried publicly on television and hung at the Forum before a hockey game and no one would give a damn but you. It means that I'm filthy and a failure, and that I've got nowhere to go and that of all the people who bump against me in the street, I've chosen to take you with me. It means I'm nothing and you're unlucky for having ended up at the desk beside mine. It means that I'm almost making myself sick with this whole silly episode."

A wave of disgust for him, for myself, for the street and its passersby had engulfed me. I don't know what I had intended to do but I couldn't go through with it. I released my grip on his shoulders. And he, now embarrassed for his display of fear, forced a laugh.

"Ha, ha! Oh, I see, some sort of joke, eh, I get it."

"That's right," I said, "some sort of joke, now go away."

Another nervous laugh and he moved quickly down the street.

VI

What was happening to me? Was anything happening to me?
Perhaps that has always been the greatest error in my life, believing that something was changing, that I was taking some new
direction. What a concept that is; what an illusion for those
bound to the wheel. There is no man who has not indulged
himself in daydreams of violence. Power through violence, what
an intoxicating dream! The regiments with your symbols on
banners, the columns of armored vehicles commanded by narrow-
eyed, serious officers paralyzing the hostile cities like so many
hypodermic needles plunged into the vital center, the personal
guard dedicated and beautiful, the youths, the songs, the armor,
the violinists, the fire on the water, the pledge, the vow, the
promise, the covenant, and I am weeping over my working
nation that I should be the instrument of all this, help me, my
lieutenants, help me to the balcony, I must thank the people,
they are standing beside the rivers weeping, weeping beside the
mountains, thank you, Arctic, thank you, orchards, thank you,

islands, thank you, iron fields, dedicated O Canada, finally dedicated, the women childbearing, flesh oiled, sails perfumed, the steaming platters on the backs of beauty, the desire, the inspection, the choice, the love, O Marylin, hold me, I am myself forever, evermore my mountain. I am sorry, I apologize, young man, book-keeper with a Plattsburg suit, forgive me, forgive me. What was happening to me? Was anything happening to me? I had intimidated a boy, frightened a boy against a brick wall. Was I a step closer to a dream? Not a dream of personal domination, a dream of the act which changes things, the significant blow which is delivered and felt, a dream of the life which finds its own level as the purest or foulest water does.

VII

I walked quickly over to the train station, which was only a few blocks from where I worked. It seemed darker than it had the night before. The loudspeaker announced the names of cities of an impossible odyssey. There is a kind of brotherhood among people in a train station, even a large station. Of course, all humans need is the vaguest thing in common to give them the opportunity of greeting one another in friendship. I've noticed among sportscar enthusiasts that even in city traffic one will hail another if he happens to be driving the same make of car. In a train station, we are all somehow associate with trains, reading schedules, watching the great clock over the information desk, greeting someone, leaving someone. It is enough to establish a bond of community. I found myself nodding and smiling at strangers as I made my way toward the baggage room.

The atmosphere of the baggage room was not at all like that of the main station, no hustle-bustle here, no determined walks or faces full of anticipation. The room was high roof, flat plaster roofs painted green. Behind a long, low metal counter were stacked rows and rows of trunks, bags, and valises. Humans do not travel lightly, I thought, they do not leave much behind, all this portable property changing cities, changing closets, changing drawers. There were several people waiting at the counter and only one baggage clerk, I noted with annoyance. He was a small man wearing thin blue suspenders over a striped green shirt. His sleeves were rolled up and I noticed he had no hair on his arms. Did he have a harelip? I saw his face for a moment and then he turned away, I could not be sure. Now he came up to the counter struggling with three valises.

"We're short today," he said to the lady to whom he presented them, "half the staff sick and all at once."

He did not have a harelip, but his mouth was twisted, the small distorted lips puffed out like a torn sail. All his features, the light blue milky eyes that blinked so often, the narrow wide-nostril nose, and the sailing mouth, they seemed concentrated in a very small area on his face, an area slightly off center which gave the impression of his looking away even when he stood directly in front of you. His skin was fair, the wrinkles around his eyes done in light brown, the color of the few large freckles on his forehead and his thinning hair. He combined in his appearance something of early youth and old age. I imagined he had looked the same way all his life. He licked his lips after each time he spoke, an unfortunate habit, I thought, for a man with a twisted mouth.

"It never rains but it pours," he said to the lady.

His face was weak and ugly, yes, ugly; I cannot refrain from applying the word to him. He dug something out of his ear and rolled it between his thumb and index finger. He wore a gold band on the wedding finger of his left hand. His hands were freckled and, strangely enough, chubby; they appeared almost too big for the rest of his body. His weak eyes gave an effeminate quality to his face and, as I have mentioned, he fairly fluttered them. What is it about our conditioning that moves us to hate the weak and ugly? What stories were we told of beautiful riders and delicate girls to make us persecutors of the lame, the coarse, and the broken? Why have we the same words to describe the beauty of the body and the beauty of the soul? Those legends of Christianity, the beauty of the oppressed and the invalid, how have they withered so totally before the striding hero? How was my heart so divided to feel such pity and such contempt the first time I had seen this ugly baggage clerk? And had I known at that moment what a part this ugly baggage clerk would come to play in my life, I would have quit that high green room at once. Although there were others who had come before me, because I was standing beside the lady for whom he had rendered his most recent service, he asked if he might help me. Then he licked his lips. His tongue was quick, finger-shaped, and bright. I said nothing and handed him my grandfather's baggage check. I could hardly bear to look at him. He took the check from me, studied it, and headed to the furthest stack of baggage. He examined a few labels and shook his head and moved to another stack. Nothing there either. His search continued over to several other stacks with no better luck. Meanwhile, some of the people waiting were becoming impatient. He returned, shaking his head.

"I'm terribly sorry, sir," he said. "I'm afraid I can't locate this piece. You'll have to take it up with the Baggage Master. He'll be back from lunch at two."

"That's impossible," I said, "I have to be back at work at two. Couldn't you just have another look? It's probably a very old valise."

"C'mon," said a tall man, "be a good fellow and let someone else have a chance; some of us were here before you."

I had no desire to antagonize the crowd there, so I took back the check, nodded to the tall man, and departed. As a matter of fact, the valise had been lost, an event the Baggage Master informed me later happened very infrequently indeed. It was difficult to ascertain the value of the bag because of the language barrier between my grandfather and I, but it was finally set at one hundred dollars. I found the whole transaction very tedious and have no intention of burdening you with any further details concerning it. I merely wanted to describe to you my first meeting with the baggage clerk, a man whose life became, for some time, as important as my own.

VIII

Returning home that evening, I reviewed the episode I had had
with the young book-keeper. Certainly, my actions were somehow
connected with the arrival of my grandfather. His assault on the
policeman had impressed me immensely. There was something
clear and correct about it, a beauty which was almost contagious.
Of course, I was not able to carry through the violence with the
young book-keeper. It hadn't meant that much to me.

I interrupted these thoughts with the sudden realization that
I could not make love to Marylin in my room because of my
grandfather's presence. I entertained several schemes for getting
him out of the room for those few hours every night. Perhaps
the landlady could amuse him in her own room as a special favor
to me, though there was no reason on earth why she should ren-
der me any special favors. Perhaps he could be trusted to spend
a few hours in the coffee shop beside the rooming house. I tried
to reckon just how long it took us to make love. *To make love,*
how distasteful that phrase was and yet it described the act quite

precisely: two people working diligently, calling on all the skills they know to produce pleasurable but ephemeral sensations. And now, our affair having already stretched into months, the work tended to become more and more dull. Perhaps I might use the pretext of my grandfather's visit to ease the pain and tedium of a separation that must eventually take place. Then the hunt would begin again, the hunt, the lure, the seduction (usually mutual), the mutual promises kept purposefully vague—the whole process wearied me even in conjecture. That is what must keep many together, I thought, just the trouble of another hunt, the tiresome prospect of repeating the old stories to new women and hearing theirs, of learning what she likes and teaching her what you like, how you want this done, how she wants that done, and all that ritual with which we surround the essential act of relief. The essential act of relief, the *purging*, the *purification*, how well those words described the feelings I felt, even though vicariously, from observing my grandfather during his few moments of glory the evening before. The landlady greeted me at the door.

"I'm worried about him, your grandfather. He lays on the bed the whole day and he doesn't move, only he moans, moans the whole day. Moans, snores, what's the difference, I ask you, when he lays all day on the bed and doesn't move?"

"Well, he's an old man, you can't expect him to skip about."

"I'm worried," she said. "I don't want anyone to die in my place, do you understand? I don't want anyone to die, it gives a place a bad name. Mrs. Raymond had someone die at her place and she couldn't rent the room for two months. Nobody wants to sleep where someone has just died. Goodness knows I wouldn't want to to lie in the same bed myself, and I'm not even superstitious. Would you? I say die in a hospital, that's the place to die, with doctors around, where nobody loses money. Mrs. Raymond knew he was sick, she told me he moaned all day, just like him inside, and she asked him to go. 'Give me a week more,' he asked, and she had to because he had already paid for it. Then he spits blood and locks the door. She bangs and bangs, but he won't let her in. She hears him singing and coughing, singing and coughing, walking up and down, not even trying to get well. 'It was like an opera,' she told me, 'but I wasn't laughing,' she said. Soon she doesn't hear nothing. A day passes, and she gets frightened and with the postman they break open the door to his room. He's dead like she figured, lying on the floor. The bedclothes are completely covered with blood, soaking with blood, it seems he didn't have no Kleenex. It gets around and she can't rent the room for two months. The mattress has got stains on it to this day. Now who's going to take a room with a mattress like that in it?"

"She finally rented it, you say."

"Finally, after two months, you know how much money that is?"

"I'm sure it's a great deal," I said, walking past her and into my room.

My grandfather was lying on my bed, dressed as when I had left him, breathing heavily and staring at the ceiling.

"What, what?" he said without turning as I entered.

I leaned over him so that he could see my face. "It's me, Grampa."

"Ah, good boy."

"Did you spend a good day, Grampa?"

No response.

Again.

"Did you spend a good day, Grampa?"

"Good, good."

He sat up abruptly and looked at me as though startled.

"Who, who are you?"

"You know me," I said, leaning very close to him. "You remember me?"

"Yes, good boy, yes. Bad to be old. Bad to be old. Forget everything."

He took my hand and smiled.

"Now, I remember."

Each word he said was important to me. In him were locked so many innocent secrets. I wanted him to continue speaking.

"Do you remember my father? Do you remember him?"

"Your father, Frederik, that was your father. My son, my young son. Wild, wild. Cart, I gave him cart and horse, red cart. Wild."

He sat up and looked at me, evidently having interested himself with those few words.

"Wild boy. In our town was a hill, big hill down to water." He described the slope with his hands. "He rides through our town, takes all the dogs and cats into cart, fills cart with cats and dogs, pulls them to top of hill and takes off horse. Big hill down to deep water. Pushes cart, all animals screaming down to deep water. He sits on top of horse on hill like army general. Into the water, bang, animals die, his cart broke. People try to whip him, he goes on horse away, away for two weeks gone."

The narrative tired the old man and he lay back on the bed.

"Did he come back?" I inquired anxiously, caught up in the story.

He shook his head up and down.

"Oh, yes, he come back. First, I pay all the people money, so they will not kill him. Then he come back on horse with woman, girl very young, very frightened. 'I marry her,' he says. Too young, he is only fifteen, girl twelve maybe. We keep them two days until I find from where comes little girl. From near town. Then at night when he sleeps, we take her back to father. Must to pay more money to him. I am rich in my town, I am butcher." He made a chopping motion with his hand. "Rich in my town, no money now, poor, poor. He shrugged his shoulders. But who cares? Poor, ha, ha." His face had brightened during the narration and at the word poor he slapped his thigh and burst out laughing. "Who cares! Who cares!"

His humor infected me, I could never explain why, and I too began laughing.

"Poor, poor, but who cares!" he said, and we followed it with nearly hysterical laughter.

"Then he tries to kill my wife, his mother," he said, suddenly serious.

"What?"

"'You take my woman,' he says, 'now I take your woman.' Tries to put pillow on her face. I have to beat him now, very hard. Wild boy, very wild but a good man, oh, a good man, I telling you. Wild boy puts all animals in new cart. In our town was hill, big hill down to water."

I let him tell the story again. How good it was to hear that heavy accent again, though I believe he spoke English more fluently than my parents. Certainly, he could communicate far more effectively. Halfway through the story for the second time, he stopped and asked, "Did I tell you this, I think I tell you this."

"Yes, you did," I said, "but I want to hear it again."

"Good, good," and he continued happily, like someone reciting an old poem for a friend's pleasure.

Later Marylin came over and I introduced her to my grand-father.

"Your wife?" he asked trying to stand up.

"Please don't disturb yourself," she said. "No, I'm not his wife, only a friend."

There was pain in her voice as she said it.

With Marylin's arrival, my grandfather became concerned with his appearance. He pulled up his tie, buttoned his vest and jacket, and tried to smooth the wrinkles in his suit, all while lying down.

"Please don't disturb yourself on my account," Marylin said gently to him.

Finally, he announced that he wanted to shave.

"Tomorrow morning, Grampa," I suggested.

"Tonight, I must shave," and he got up from the bed. "You have razor?"

I followed him into the bathroom and showed him my razor, an old-fashioned safety with a two-piece head. I started to unscrew it to replace the blade, but he grabbed it from my hand and said, "I know how, go back to lady."

I hurried back to the room, anxious to embrace her. She held me very tightly. I noticed stains on her collar. Her hair smelt fresh, she had just washed it, I supposed.

"Marylin, I don't know what we're going to do now, I mean, where we're going to go with my grandfather living here now."

She avoided the problem.

"He seems like a fine old man," she said.

"If only you didn't live with a roommate."

Then she said, a little bitterly, "We don't have to sleep together every night. I don't think either of us will disintegrate if we abstain for a few nights."

It is beginning, I thought, now it is beginning, the slow diminishing and the slow separation. I looked at her hair, sifting it through my fingers like fine falling sand.

"Don't do that," she said, drawing away.

"Don't do what?"

"Handle my hair that way. You look like a head-hunter inspecting a victim before the operation."

"Perhaps you would rather I didn't touch you at all with all your talk about simple abstention."

I moved close to her and used my knee to my advantage. I have always admired her quick sexual response, I have never tired of it.

"No, no, never touch me," she whispered heavily in my ear. "I wish that we were, my beloved, white birds on the foam of the sea."

As she became excited, she usually became more eloquent and literary. I maneuvered her to the bed.

"Your grandfather," she said.

"He's shaving. We have time."

She immediately stiffened and withdrew from me.

"Just a quickie, is that it, is that what you men call it? Oh, God," she said, crossing to the windows over which I had drawn the shades. "We have time, we have time, we could just manage it, couldn't we? I am haunted by numberless islands and many a Canaan shore where Time would surely forget us, and Sorrow come no more; soon far from the rose and the lily, and the fret of flames we would be where we were only white birds, my beloved, buoyed out on the foam of the sea. Does my body haunt you like those numberless islands?"

"Why are you starting this? I wanted you, that's all. Is there anything wrong with that?" I asked.

"Yes, yes, I know you only wanted to love me in an old high way. You laid the spices around me, the perfume, the lace, you crushed the poem into my hand with the flowers you had swum the rapids to fetch. Is this all there is to it, it is just an embrace and a farewell between us?"

That's it exactly, I thought sadly to myself. That's it exactly, a blind embrace in a city street and farewell waved through a shuttered window. "What else do you want?" I wanted to shout, "what else can I give you?"

"Isn't there any love, isn't there such a thing, not the love of two fugitives who happen to trip over each other in a sewer, but something that is sought and found and acclaimed and confirmed?"

"I told you I loved you."

"A dialogue between two fugitives."

"I suppose that is all that it meant to you, something that you could throw at me in one of your speeches."

"Oh, no, please no. I valued and treasured those words, I swear I did. They were the most important words ever told to me." She stopped speaking suddenly and rubbed her face with her open palm. "I'm sorry," she said, "forgive me. I suppose that I was upset that you wanted me quickly before we had hardly greeted each other." She crossed back into my arms.

"Forgive me," she said again.

"It is my fault, it's my fault, you are right. Next time, I will court you."

She smiled, which encouraged me.

"I'll court you with perfume and spices and lace, and crush into your hand the poem and the flowers I had crossed the water-falls to fetch. I do love you, Marylin, I do."

I should not have said that to her. I should have said, "Leave me, leave me, I am haunted by a woman's body, but it doesn't matter whose." I should have said, "I do not understand you, I do not understand a thing you have said, you do not live in my world." I should have said, "I am unworthy of you because you want love and I do not know what I want."

"I love you, Marylin," I said again.

She held me tightly. Her hair smelled of perfume. There was a stain on her collar. Her arms encircled my neck and she hung like some proud bird I had slain.

"Thank you," she said, "Oh, thank you."

The flush of a toilet, the opening of a door and a scream from the landlady. Marylin and I rushed into the hall. The landlady was standing beside my grandfather. His face was streaming with blood, his hands (one of which was still holding the razor), were covered with blood, the towel around his neck was stained with great dark blotches. My immediate thought was that he had attempted suicide.

"Blood!" the landlady cried. "Just like Mrs. Raymond, she warned me, don't let him lie down, don't let him near the mattress!"

My grandfather looked at her and shrugged his shoulders. She was speaking too quickly for him. He was smiling like a confused child close to tears, close to laughter, his eyes wet and sparkling through the soap and blood. He held out the razor towards me. In changing the blade, he had neglected to screw back the bottom piece of the razor head, so he had tried to shave with a naked blade.

"Razor no good."

I took it from him and pushed him into the bathroom. Marylin wet a towel and dabbed his face with it. The cuts were not deep, but they were numerous. He had probably shaved most of his face before he discovered something was wrong.

"Forgive," he said, "so much to trouble you."

After repeated applications of the cold wet towel the bleeding had all but stopped and we led him back to the bed.

"Put some newspapers under him," said the landlady who in the meantime had mopped up the drops of blood which had splattered the floor. "The poor man." She crushed by us in the doorway and spread the bed with newspapers.

He lay down, cleared his nasal passage, and looked for somewhere to spit. I supplied a handkerchief.

"I should have watched him," I said guiltily, "he could have hacked himself to pieces."

From that time on, I shaved my grandfather myself. In the next few weeks, I learned with a growing sense of pity towards him how dirty old men could be. One meal or defecation could be disastrous for a suit of clothes. A sneeze could ruin a shirt. Razors, stairs, mirrors, curbs were all hazards. The landlady surveyed the scene for a few moments and when she was certain he was not endangering her mattress, she left the room.

"Wild boy," my grandfather began. "'You take my woman,' he says, 'I take yours.' On top of the hill like a general and all the animals squealing. I have to beat him, I cut stick and beat him. Soon I give him new cart."

Soon he was asleep. I turned off the lights and Marylin and I lay on the other bed. Every time my grandfather moved the newspapers thundered around him. I told Marylin about my grandfather's assault on the policeman and my episode with the young book-keeper.

"We are all close to violence," she said. "It always seems like such an honest path through the tangles of humiliation."

"Was I humiliated by that nauseating young man?"

"I think you were," she said, tracing the features of my face lightly with her hand. "I think that simply you were hurt by his observations about your clothes and your position. We see violence all around us; bombs, auto accidents, concentration camp crematoria, easily integrated in our memory; it's such a familiar thing, I wonder why more people don't resort to it to settle their accounts."

I knew most of the clothes she owned, their buttons, strings, and snaps, and I undressed her easily. I had promised to make a courtly love to her.

"Your body always surprises me."

I lied. Her body no longer surprised me. I knew all its secrets. It was lying naked in my prison, languishing there, until the rest of her pilgrim lovers would discover her and be surprised. I thought of those lovers, countless thighs and breasts, countless bodies in their history who would still gasp in surprise at her first unclothing as they had for all the first unclothings in their long journeys.

"Marylin, I love your thighs, I can never quite believe their shape, they are like lovely continents for exploration."

I lied. Never before had her thighs been so mortally made of flesh and bone and blood. I swear I could feel them dying under my mouth and hands.

"Your hands."

I lied, I lied. Why hadn't she a special body for love, one that bloomed at night like a strange flower? Why did she offer me this body, that she used all day, which worked, sweated, eliminated, ached? And so, I lied and lied, taking her breathing body deeper and deeper toward the deepest lie, the climax of lies when her body arched and shuddered and then slowly resumed reality, putting it on like clothes.

"Thank you," she whispered, "you are so good to me, you took me so completely."

Later, as if she had been reading my thoughts with a reversing mirror, she said, "Oh, God, isn't it beautiful that we can do this together with our everyday bodies, which carry us to and from work, and with our everyday minds?"

"Yes. Yes."

And I thought of Canada, no patriot, but awestruck at its sudden size stretching out, beyond the flesh I stroked in falsity, beyond the containing room which smothered me with my lies, I thought of Canada abandoning my body to Marylin, sending my mind out with a *Pax vobiscum* along the sparse strand of darkening cities to the heaving Pacific, north to the frozen bodies of slain animals, bloodless in the white cold night through numberless islands, coursing in huge continental rivers, plunging in forests of ancient trees, sleeping on the naked plain and under the growing mountains. My grandfather thundered and crashed on his newspaper sheet.

"I love you," I told Marylin, "I love you, I love you."

"I love you," she said.

IX

During the next few weeks, I continued to make love to Marylin. Each evening, we would wait until my grandfather fell asleep and then we would begin. Sometimes, he would wake up, wanting to know where he was, and I would leave Marylin's side, thankful for the interruption, and reassure the old man. A doctor came to give him a check-up and he told me that my grandfather was afflicted with nothing but old age and advised me to make life as easy for him as possible. The financial strain was not too great. I bought him a few shirts, he borrowed some of my clothes, and he ate very little. Of course, the cleaning bill rose. I did begin to miss my privacy and I began taking walks by myself through the city whenever I could manage. These were not happy weeks for me. I suppose I did not feel the loss of privacy, as acutely as I might have, because of the overwhelming sense of guilt I felt in my relationship with Marylin. I could not bring myself to break with her. For some deep reason, which I could not fathom, I needed her. Or perhaps the reason was not so deep at all. Perhaps I was afraid of

the loneliness which would ensue. Perhaps I was afraid of breaking a ritual, of losing something which I had. I think that I ceased
to think altogether. The little imaginings, which had given me
so much pleasure before, now never even seemed to occur.
Each morning, I rose after a heavy sleep, and after I had prepared
breakfast for my grandfather and myself, I shaved the old man
while he told me stories. All day, I was employed by Mr. Rand, the
young book-keeper religiously avoiding me, and in the evenings,
I was employed by Marylin. My grandfather spent most of his
time on his bed. I had forgotten his spectacular arrival. I had no
thought of violence or anything else for that matter. After a few
days, I did not even resent Marylin, I merely became numb to
her. I went through my lines and was happy when sleep came.

One day after work, I was visiting the bookstores on Ste.
Catherine Street before returning to the rooming house and
eventually to Marylin. I browsed about, picking up this and that,
feeling a vague pleasure in my leisure as the crowds outside were
hurrying home. I searched mostly in the second-hand sections of
these stores among those foolish, pompous, serious, and obscure
volumes which no one wished to keep, books on the nature of
God by American ministers, books on nature by millionaires,
travel books like *By Foot through Nova Scotia*, political solutions by
second rate theorists: *Universalism, the Ideal State*, books of appre-
ciation, instruction, and charming madness. Across the aisle,
I saw a man whose mouth was twisted, the small distorted lips
puffed out like a torn sail. It was the baggage clerk. At the sight
of his face, which can only be described as weak and ugly, a sharp
sensation of hate surged through my body. Actually, I quivered.
It was the first intense sensation I had experienced in some
time and I distinctly remember enjoying it. He seemed nervously
involved in some book, but I could not tell what it was from

where I stood. Carefully, I walked by him and stood behind him. It was a book of Boccaccio illustrated by Rockwell Kent. He was not reading it but thumbing through from one illustration to another. He studied each heavy-lined erotic picture and I even saw him run his hand over one. The sensation of hate I had first experienced on sighting him did not diminish, rather it increased and became more pleasurable. I moved into a position where I could see his face. He was gloating over a shining nude cornered by a black-robed monk. He licked his lips, his face dedicated in sensual interest, and turned the page reluctantly. What delight we derive from observing the ugly perform in ugliness. I hated him righteously and perfectly as though all evil, hypocrisy, and shame lived in that weak body, behind that distorted face and nowhere else.

I followed him out of that bookstore and into another close by. Here, he looked at the photography and art magazines filled with pictures of nudes. I observed his orgy with the secret joy and contempt the pure have for the degraded. I felt as though I had been chosen for a mission, that my stumbling upon this man had been no accident, that we had been prepared for this day. A quiet came over, a calm I had not experienced for weeks, and a smile held my mouth. He had been delivered to me, my victim, my test, my salvation, and because of that raging hatred within me I sensed a profound love for him. My little victim, my dear victim, my precious victim. He must be protected and saved for me alone. After having studied five or six magazines, he went out into the street again. I followed him. At one corner he bought a *Montreal Daily Star*. He did not even look at the headline but tucked it under his arm. At another newsstand, he bought a copy of a notorious tabloid which flashed the thick headline

MONSTER ASSAULTS MOTHER. Ashamed of his most recent purchase, he wrapped the larger *Montreal Star* around it. I walked a few feet behind him along Ste. Catherine Street and up Peel Street, which is only one street east of my own room. He climbed the stairs of a rooming house and fumbled in his pocket for the key, I suppose.

"Wait," I called from the street, "wait."

"Are you talking to me?" he asked as I climbed the stairs three steps at a time.

"That's right," I said with a smile. "I'm talking to you."

I stood before him, shaking my head slowly up and down.

"I have something to tell you."

"Something to tell me?" he said curiously and a little frightened. "And haven't I seen you somewhere before?"

"You have seen me somewhere before but that doesn't matter."

He licked his lip.

"I watched you in the bookstores," I said.

"You what?" he blurted, the fear beginning in his eyes and working down to his mouth, stiffening the flesh.

"I watched you in the bookstores. I watched you study the filthy pictures. I watched you run your hand over a picture of a monk embracing a naked woman. I watched you turn the pages of six so-called art magazines."

He did not move or speak. I stepped closer to him.

"And I watched you buy this and wrap it in the *Star*."

I pulled the roll of newspapers from under his arm. I tore off pages of the *Star* until I had exposed the tabloid. The pages fluttered from the balcony to the street.

"I mean this. MONSTER ASSAULTS MOTHER."

"Hey, you can't do this," he stuttered and licked his lips.

"Of course, I can't," I laughed, slapping his face with the tabloid. "Of course, I can't. Tell me, doesn't that lip of yours hurt you? Does it give you much pain being twisted like it is?"

"Huh, huh, huh," he gasped, completely terrorized. He searched desperately in his pocket for the key. "Huh, huh."

"Doesn't it hurt you when you eat or talk? Do your women like to kiss it? That's it, that's it, do your women like to kiss it?"

He got the key into the lock and struggled with it, shoulder against the door, it opened suddenly and he hurtled into the dark hall.

"Don't forget this," I called, throwing the tabloid after him.

He threw himself against the door and slammed it. I descended the stairs slowly and walked to my room, dedicated, intense, indifferent to the people streaming by me.

X

The landlady was waiting for me on the balcony. She started speaking before I had reached her.

"He's got to go, your grandfather, he's got to go. After what he did, I can't have him here another day. What do you think I am? I'm somebody. I'm not going to take that from him, from a nobody, from a dirty old man. Get him out of here, a man like that."

"Just a moment," I said. "What is the matter? What happened?"

"I'm not going to tell you, I'm too ashamed to repeat it. He's got to go, I can't have him here."

"If you would just tell me what he did, we could discuss it and make sure it never happens again. Maybe we could even make some new arrangement with the rent."

That broke the silence.

"With the rent?" she asked.

"Well, if he really is too much trouble for you, then perhaps a dollar or two extra a week could make it worth your while."

I had no intention of paying her anything extra unless it was really something extraordinary that the old man had done.

"Now tell me, what did he do?"

"He's dirty," she said, "he can't control himself. I go into the room this morning to make his bed, yours too like I always do, lots of landladies don't make the beds, you know. I come to make the bed I tell him, now I know he don't understand English, but he knows what I'm there for because I do the same thing every morning. But he don't get out of the bed. I figure maybe he's tired or something, so I go over to him to help him out. Then he throws it at me."

"Throws what at you?"

"I can't tell you."

"Now, I thought we decided that nothing could be done unless you told me the whole story. What did he throw at you?"

"I can't tell you. I don't know the name for it."

"You don't know the name for what?"

"What he threw."

"This is ridiculous," I said. "I'll go in and ask him myself."

"O.K., O.K.," she said, "I'll tell you. Shit."

"What?"

"He threw shit at me. He shits in his bed and I try to get him up, he throws it at me, right in my face."

I laughed, I couldn't but help seeing the humor in it.

"Oh," she said, "you laugh too, just like him. Well, the both of you can just get out of here. With you and that girl carrying on like you do, it's a wonder the police aren't down on me. What do you think I'm running here anyway? This place got a good name."

"I'm sorry for laughing, I really am, but you must admit there is something funny in the story."

"Sure, sure. If you think it's so funny you can go in there and clean it up. I'm not going to."

She tried to speak fiercely, but I could see that even she, who had been victimized, had begun to see the humor. I had to be decent about it and I told her that I would pay an extra dollar a week.

"I don't know why I stand it," she said.

My room smelt terribly. My grandfather was dressed, seated in the chair before the window. The smell emanated from a corner of the room where the dirty sheets and his pyjamas were heaped.

"I see out window you speak with her," he said.

"Don't worry, Grampa, it's forgotten now."

I carefully gathered the soiled things together, took them outside and dumped them in the garbage can.

"That's the two of my sheets you owe me for now," called the landlady after me. "That'll be five dollars at least."

"But they were used."

"What's the difference? I've got to replace them, don't I? And I wouldn't had to if it wasn't for him."

"Alright."

The truth was that my mind was reviewing, with great pleasure, the episode with my baggage clerk and nothing could dislocate that pleasure.

When I returned to the room, my grandfather said, "She no told you true."

"What do you mean?"

"Sit, listen," he said. "Old man, I crap in bed, not good, but old man no help. Comes in the landlady. I am shame her so I no wish to get out of bed. She thinks I am to play a trick, funny thing.

She thinks I mean something different. She sits on bed, beside me, takes my hand, puts it here on her." He touched my leg. "I not mind, I move hand where she tells me. It is good I think, she is old, but good, and I also am old. Then quickly, she stops my hand and stands she up. 'Terrible smell,' she says. 'What is terrible smell? Dirty man,' she says, 'dirty old man.' 'Whore,' I say to her, 'you are old whore.' She hit my face, and I reach in bed and throw crap at her face. That is true story. She run from room and after I get dressed and I clean room."

The old whore, I smiled to myself, the old whore and the democracy of lust. I couldn't take the episode seriously.

"I think you acted like a perfect gentleman," I told him, but he didn't understand. "You were right," I told him, simplifying.

"Ah," he said, "funny thing."

I opened the door and saw the landlady who had been listening to us.

"I suppose that you're going to believe that dirty old man," she said.

"I don't appreciate you listening at the door," I said firmly.

"Go way, old whore," called my grandfather from the chair.

"This is my place!" she shouted. "You can't talk to me that way, neither of you."

My grandfather laughed and made an obscene sign with his hands. The landlady swore the two of us would be out of her place before the night was over.

My grandfather laughed, "Old whore."

I was happy to see him in such good spirits. His enthusiasm corresponded with the vitality I had drawn from confronting the baggage clerk.

"Let's have a little quiet up there," called another boarder from down the hall.

"The Hell with all of you!" she yelled, slamming my door and stalking off to her room.

While I waited for Marylin to come, I chatted with the old man as he liked me to do, inquiring about the day he had spent, his health.

"Not so good, my dear." He had taken to calling me my dear and my darling. "Not so good. Soon I will die, I am too old for everything. Too old for war and too old for women. Too old to fight because I do not know how it is to rest. My country was big, no one could travel it. And my lake, only one man swimmed it. After I say to him, I cannot swim lake, but I can beat you. He does not understand why it is I must to fight him. Because we are men and no one else swims lake but you, so I must to beat you some way."

"I understand, I understand," I said with excitement. "He had to be beaten because he was victorious, because he had become an impossible example to emulate, he had to be beaten to prove that we all are men, to prove that we are all foul and glorious, victorious and degraded, not one man foul and the other glorious but each man in himself foul and glorious."

"What, what?" Of course, he hadn't understood anything I'd said.

"Tell me Grampa, did you beat him?"

"He was only man to swim over the big lake. He beat me hard, hard, nose, face, everywhere."

"He beat you? No, he couldn't have, you must have beaten him."

"Look, my darling, I like to tell you different, but he beat me."

"Well, I won't be beaten."

"What?"

"Nothing."

I emptied out the bowl where my grandfather had finally been trained to spit. Suddenly, I felt a desire to be near my baggage clerk, to watch him move and lick his lip, to delight in his loathsomeness and, with the desire, a love deeper than any I had ever felt before. Where was he now, what was he doing? In one of the rooms of Peel Street, was a woman feeding him, watching him manipulate his nourishment between his crooked lips, those exquisite deformed lips? Was she wondering what she was doing there with that weak man with the freckled baby skin, and the features concentrated and pushed to one side, so it seemed like he never looked straight at you? How well did she know that tongue, quick like a serpent, finger-shaped, and bright? Did she know the buds on that tongue and perish in them like craters when he kissed her? Or did she live a lie like so many do, imagining her husband average in an ugly world? I heard Marylin come in, but I remained in the bathroom staring into the gleaming porcelain bowl where the spit hung like white moss in the water. I flushed the toilet and ruined the garden in a vortex. Actually, I think I muttered "farewell."

Marylin was talking to my grandfather when I entered the room. She got up and embraced me and I kissed her on the mouth. She must know, I thought to myself, she must know that I don't feel anything. But she did not know, she did not wish to know. She prepared dinner for us and fed us, already moving around the room like a wife and mother, urging this morsel on my grandfather, this extra helping on me, not really listening to anything I said, but completely abandoned to the comfortable ritual of domesticity. I had let her assume this role, even approved of her assuming it because—well, I am not sure. All I can tell you is that I let her invade my life, perhaps out of indifference, perhaps out of fear. If she had not been blinded by her successes, she could have perceived that I had ceased to think or feel and that I accepted her with the same enthusiasm that I accepted the buildings and the walls.

"I missed you today," she said later. "Each person I served today, I wanted to break the salesgirl customer relationship and take her hand and say, 'Look lady, look at me, a man loves me, a man told me he loved me last night.'"

I hadn't the strength to tell her yet, to tell her to leave me, to tell her I was weary of her, to tell her I knew nothing about her. My automatic responding system went into operation.

"Marylin, I missed you too, the day dragged on and on."

And our talk dragged on and on, until my grandfather was asleep, until she was in my arms and I was telling her that I loved her, that I needed to be with her. She was lying very still beside me, my body hers, my mind persecuting my victim.

"Marriage." Had she said the word, or had I? I didn't know or care. "Yes, yes, that's what I've always wanted, to be with you." Who was speaking, I wondered vaguely?

She shook me. "Am I dreaming?" she laughed. "Am I dreaming? Is it true?"

"Of course, it's true," I said gently.

She lay beside me a long while. I felt tears on my chest.

"Are you crying?"

"Yes, because I'm so happy. You've made me so happy by wanting me."

"I've always wanted you."

Later, she said, "I want to tell someone, Oh, please, let me tell someone."

"We'll tell my grandfather, we'll wake him up and tell him."

We dressed swiftly and silently, and then switched on the lights. My grandfather moaned. I put my hand on his shoulder and shook him gently. He sat up suddenly in his bed, shielding his eyes with his hands. He ripped my hand from his shoulder and began a mounting moan like a mourning widow.

"No, no, leave me, leave me."

"What is it, Grampa? There's nothing to be alarmed about."

"Oh, forgive me, I think something else."

Marylin sat down on his bed and took his hand. "We're going to be married, your grandson and I. Isn't it wonderful?"

"What? You marry?"

"Yes," we said together, "we're going to be married."

"This is good, very good. It is not good to be so much time together and no marry. I hear you every night beside me and it is no good. What are they doing? I think. They are young, they have so much future, what are they doing? I think. They are young, they have so much future, what are they doing? Now Marylin and my dear are to marry, this is good."

Marylin blushed for the first time since I had known her. She leaned over and kissed my grandfather on the forehead. "May I call you Grampa, too? I never had a grandfather that I remember."

"Ya, you call me Grampa."

I noted a sensation of disgust. The whole scene was becoming maudlin.

"Let's tell the landlady," I suggested.

"It's two o'clock in the morning," Marylin said.

"All the better," I said.

We went down the hall together and knocked at her door, both of us giggling.

"What is it?" she called from inside, her voice guided by sleep.

"It's me, dearest landlady," I cried, "your favourite roomer."

"For Christ's sake, can't you leave me alone? It's the middle of the night."

"We must tell you something," I insisted. "It's the beginning of my life."

We heard her slouch toward us and open the door.

"Have you people gone crazy?"

"Of course we have," said Marylin, "we're going to be married."

The landlady stood in the open doorway dressed in a ridiculous red bathrobe. She tilted her head to one side like a terrier and began to smile, genuinely touched by our announcement.

"Why, that's wonderful, that's wonderful for you kids."

She embraced Marylin and was about to embrace me, but I backed away.

"I'm not going to eat you," she said.

"I can't be too sure," I said, and we all laughed.

"Since you two have got me up, what do you say we have a drop to celebrate?"

"A drop?" said Marylin. "By all means."

"By all means, indeed," I said.

"And maybe the old boy wants some too, let's take it in there, besides, we might wake someone up down here and it's hard enough already to find boarders."

"We have glasses," said Marylin, "let's go."

The landlady bore the bottle of scotch like a precious scroll, dancing like a rabbi of some obscure happy sect.

We followed after her, single file, chanting, "Here Comes the Bride."

"Shh," said the landlady.

My grandfather quickly entered into the jovial mood. He even kissed the hand of the landlady and she made a sweeping curtsy. Marylin poured out four drinks and we waited for my grandfather to make the toast, which he did in his European language.

"Now," he said, "I tell same thing in English, you forgive my English. Father and mother is happy. Man and bride is happy. Animals in field, birds in trees, all happy. The babies, soon to come, is weeping in the blackness."

"That's beautiful," Marylin said.

"Well, come on everybody, drink up," said the landlady. "How do they say: the night is young, and you are beautiful?"

"Everyone is beautiful, but he is the most beautiful of all," Marylin said, raising my hand like a champion prizefighter.

"Aw shucks," I said.

"A living doll," the landlady said.

Marylin sat close to me. The glasses were filled and refilled. Another bottle was discovered in the landlady's room, and though it was only half full, it was greeted like the birth of a saviour.

"'*Methought a Voice within the Tavern cried,*'" Marylin said, and with academic pomposity, added, "The fifth edition of the translation."

"I suppose you believed I thought it was only the third," I said solemnly suspicious. "Of course, the fifth."

She kissed my hand. The landlady had become a ballerina. She held the corners of her red bathrobe like wings, spun in a diminishing circle fluttering these cloth wings and finally collapsed in a heap on the floor.

"Bravo, bravo," my grandfather applauded, and he leaned over and slapped her buttocks.

"Make bigger circles," said the landlady, not moving.

"Now, now," said Marylin, helping her up, "we mustn't encourage them, or we'll be ravished in broad daylight."

"You are absolutely right," said the landlady, "another invitation and they'll be on top of us."

"A girl can't be too careful," Marylin said.

Then it was my grandfather's turn. He stood up and with a gallant bow invited Marylin to dance.

"La, la, la, La, la, la," sang the landlady, advancing to me with outstretched arms. "La, la, la, La, la, la."

"I think I'll sit this one out, if you don't mind," I said.

Undismayed by my refusal, the landlady shrugged her shoulders, took my grandfather's pillow for a partner, and danced dizzily beside the other couple.

"La, lala, la, lala."

"What the hell," I said, and I got up and caught her hands, the pillow falling to the floor. We tripped over it as I whirled her in my arms.

"The Danube is blue-ue-ue ue," I sang.

"And I like to screw-ew ew-ew ew," injected the landlady.

Then the four of us joined hands in a circle.

"Hush-a, hush-a, all fall down," sang Marylin and we all fell down.

The windows had begun to brighten, and I decided to take Marylin home.

"Don't worry about us oldies," said the landlady moving on the bed beside my grandfather. "We can take care of ourselves. Get it?"

My grandfather was lying beside her, exhausted by the dance.

"Old whore," he said, and slapped her seat.

Marylin and I walked to her apartment. I wondered what I was doing beside her. It seemed as though we had just attended someone else's party and that it had been pleasant enough. She clung tightly to my arm, irritating a pimple with her pressing thumb.

"That was the nicest party I'll ever have," she said.

"We're going to be married, Betty, we're going to be married," she said, shaking her sleeping roommate.

Betty woke up. It was the first time I had ever seen her. She seemed younger than Marylin and certainly more beautiful.

"Oh, isn't that wonderful," she said, hopping out of bed and hugging Marylin. Her breasts were clearly visible through her nightgown. "I'm so happy for the both of you."

She kissed me, and I remember thinking simply that I wanted her. Marylin walked me to the door and came into the hall with me.

"We'll work together, we'll build something together," she said. "We'll make a lie of all the sad poems of betrayal and death."

"I know we will," I said, "I know we can."

"Isn't it stupid?" she said. "I feel like a child bride, like a virgin."

She leaned her head against my chest.

"No, it isn't stupid," I responded automatically, "it's very beautiful."

"Do you feel like a virgin?" she asked in a soft child's voice.

"Yes, in a way I do, like I've found a new virginity."

"Yes," she said, "I know what you mean, it's a kind of virginity that only the degraded can come upon and, because of that, it's somehow sweeter. A virginity that stands for achievement and not abstinence."

At that moment, I wanted to cast her aside, to free myself forever from the impossible burden of her love. I wanted to tell her of *my* new virginity, of *my* new purity of dedication, but I did not yet have the strength. Soon, I would have the strength, my victim would give it to me, his ugliness would fill me with it and his shame sustain it. And I was weary of her, she who had no place in this mission, who led me by my weak hand into lies and deceit. When would I have the strength to tell her to leave me?

"Suddenly, I feel so clean," she said, "our love makes me feel so clean."

"O God," I screamed silently in desperation. "How can you be so blind? How are you so weak as to let me do this to you? Why don't you resist me? Why do you make me make you suffer? Why are you compelling me to hurt you?"

"So do I," I said, kissing her.

"It's almost day," she said. "I'll be dead tomorrow, but I won't care. Goodnight! Remember I love you. Will you remember?"

"Of course I will remember, goodnight Marylin. Aren't you going in?"

"I want to see you go, I want to see you walk down the hall."

"Alright," I laughed, "I will see you tomorrow."

It was almost dawn. The waking birds had no traffic to compete with and their filibuster was steady and loud. The days were getting warmer and warmer. In the soft morning light, the city looked as though it had been carved out of a dark pearl. I did not go home immediately. I walked over to Peel Street and stood facing the rooming house where the man, who was becoming so important in my life, was sleeping. I was not tired in the least. I wanted to see him. And I had to find out his name. I needed his name for comfort and excitement, to speak to myself as a charm and formula. I climbed the stairs of my own rooming house and as I opened the door, I heard a frightened shuffle from my room. I paused in the vestibule to give the landlady an opportunity of making a graceful escape. The door of my room opened slowly, her head emerged, and seeing no one, she fled down the hall to her room adjusting her nightgown with her free hand as she ran, holding her red bathrobe in the other. My grandfather was sleeping deeply, his pyjamas flung on the floor beside the bed. "Old flesh," I said to myself, covering his body.

The alcohol smell was strong in the room and I was grateful for it. I did not want to smell his skin or the lingering odor of the landlady's dying flesh. I opened the good window and poked out the cardboard which replaced the glass my grandfather had smashed. With pleasure, I remembered that gesture and I reflected on how much the old man had taught me already. It seemed as though it was he who had delivered the baggage clerk into my hands, and though he knew nothing of the afternoon's episode, I had felt his guidance all through the action. It was he who had taught me to act swiftly and decisively. Why hadn't I appreciated him these past few weeks? How could I have thought him dull? Even with his language difficulty, he was more articulate than anyone I knew. I marvelled at his supreme insult to the landlady who had humiliated him, throwing his own excrement in her face. Disgusting, yes, but also a clear hard act and there is some-thing in that alone, in this world of bickering and vagueness. I slept for an hour until the alarm rang.

While we breakfasted, my grandfather said, "It is good you marry. Not good to be alone. I was alone too long."

"Look, Grampa, I might as well tell you this now." I spoke very slowly so that he could understand everything I said. "I am not really sure I want to marry her."

"You have fear, it is hard."

"No, it's not that I'm frightened, that I have fear, I do not think that I love her."

"You not love her," he said. "I think this is true. Sometimes you do not put out every light and I see you when you are with her. You do not see me. You think me sleep. I pretend so I should not to give you shame. I know you got no money to go somewhere else. I see your face when you hold her. It is full with pain, like man with heavy sickness."

"What do you think that I should do, Grampa?"

He smacked his open hand down on the table, upsetting an empty glass. "You must to send her away. Finish. You must now to kill it. You not love her, must to say goodbye. Finish." He stood up, pointing his finger at me over the table, and almost shouting. "Your father, wild father, we had lock on his door, every night we must to lock his door and lock the horse. He want to ride to get twelve years girl. We catch him many times. Beat him. No good. After two years, he ride to her, and she is his wife soon. This is love, understand? He want her hard, hard."

My grandfather sat down on his bed, breathing heavily. Of course, he was right. I must finish with Marylin as soon as possible. But I must confess that even at that moment when we were discussing her, she was not foremost in my thoughts. In fact, it seemed as though my rejection of Marylin he had already accepted as a foregone conclusion and that now he was urging me to accept a new kind of purity. Finish. Begin again. Finish. Begin again.

While I was shaving him, he said, "You must to tell her soon."

"Yes, yes," I agreed.

"Good boy."

I dragged the razor like a plough through the soap on his face, his old skin gleaming between the walls of snow. In the furrows of his face, there were narrow orchards of bristles protected each day from the blade by their depth. My grandfather sat on the toilet seat, very erect during the operation, as if he had always been used to personal barbers. Leaving for work, I saw the landlady in the hall.

"About that extra dollar a week," I said.

"O.K., O.K.," she said, "I get it. Forget it."

"Perhaps you should pay us something," I suggested humorously.

"Who do you think he is, Valentino? He fell asleep halfway. But he's alright for an old fellow."

"I'm sure you'll be very happy together," I said.

In the street a pang of longing possessed me, a need to be in the presence of my victim so profound that I decided not to go to work but to go immediately to the train station.

XI

Once I was in the station, I did not go directly to the baggage room. I was close enough to him to starve myself exquisitely. I sat down on a wooden bench in the waiting room and watched the people around me. I fingered through the magazines at the stand. I studied a train schedule at the information booth. Finally, I sickened myself with these diversions. *Why was I making a game of this?* I asked myself severely. I was not persecuting him for myself only; this was above the personal. I tried to recall those feelings of dignity and mission which I had felt the afternoon before when he had fled from me into his dark hall. How hard it was to recall them. How destructive had been the single evening of lies with Marylin. Purity, a life must be pure, a search after purity. Contamination was so easy and so dangerous. And with the terrible power of words themselves, by concentrating on purity, dignity, dedication, by saying them slowly, kissing the first syllable of purity with full lips, gulping, bathing my throat with the deep g of dignity, rebuked by the thud of my tongue against the roof of my mouth, while I explored dedication, I felt myself being slowly cleansed. My heart racing, I went to the baggage room. I did not forget my exercises as I walked. Purity, dignity, dedication. I saw him there. He looked whole and undiseased. He was not marked with shame except the sustaining shame of his ugliness. I surrendered myself to the overwhelming excitement of hate and love and ecstasy. *Oh, God,* I cried in the hollows of my soul, *it is before the fire that men are tried.* Nothing else matters but the hours before the fire. I had never been impure, I had never been turned from my purpose. Here I was, in my work, in my love, and I had never been anywhere else. I do not know how long I watched him; perhaps two hours, perhaps three. I stood half obscured by a pillar and he did not see me. If people brushed by me, I did not notice them.

Then, he left the baggage room and went through a door in the room behind it marked *For Employees Only.* After he was gone a few moments, I climbed over the low steel counter and followed him into the bathroom. No one stopped me. He was the only one in the bathroom. The antiseptic smell, the gleaming white tile made this room appropriate for the drama which was about to ensue. He was seated in the third cubicle, his trousers accordioned around his ankles. The light above betrayed him. His shadow lapped his ankles like a small dark pool. He was masturbating. I leaned against the polished wall, waiting for him. The chrome taps, the white wet bowls, the neat cubicles, all seemed instruments of purification or persuasion. I filled a sink with cold water and bathed my hands until they were numb. The shadow lurched and changed as he stood up. I heard him snap his suspenders over his shoulders. He pulled open the door and emerged.

"Not you!" he said in a high voice, licking his lips.

His face was white, and he was trembling. I do not think I will ever see another face so contorted in sheer terror. His own ugliness, his guilt and fright transformed his face into a terrible and loathsome beauty.

"You were masturbating," I said.

"Leave me alone!" he cried, lunging for the door.

I was swifter, and he crashed against my chest.

"Don't touch me!" I commanded.

He stepped back automatically, his hands hanging limply.

"Why?" he said pathetically, his voice hardly a breath.

"Yes," I said, "why?" I pointed to the cubicle where he had performed. "Is this a regular morning ritual?"

"Let me go, please, let me go."

"Didn't you hear my question? I asked you if this was a regular morning ritual?"

He was incapable of answering. The surprise had been too great. He had lapsed into a kind of shock. Could I afford to touch him? "*For whatsoever man he be that hath a blemish, he shall not approach: a blind man or a lame, or he that hath a flat nose, or anything superfluous.*" The memory of an old chapter and an old book, the words rolled before my mind like an opening scroll. "*Or a man that is broken footed, or broken handed, or crookback, or a dwarf, or be scurvy, or be scabbed. He shall not defile himself. He shall be holy unto thee, neither shall he go into any dead body, neither shall he go out of the sanctuary.*" "No," I cried. "Those are old, those commandments are too old." I wanted to slap my victim, to end his escape into shock. Those commandments are too old, we cannot be pure in the sanctuary; it is only among lepers that we can be pure. "*When a man shall have in the skin of his flesh a rising, a scab or a bright spot, and it shall be in the skin of his flesh like the plague of leprosy, then he shall be brought unto the priest. And the priest shall look on the plague in the skin of the flesh: and when the hair in the plague is turned white, and the plague in sight be deeper than the skin of his flesh, it is a plague of leprosy: and the priest shall look on him and pronounce him unclean.*" "Unclean!" I shouted. "No," I cried to myself, "those are old, those commandments are too old." "*And he entered again into the synagogue: and there was a man there which had a withered hand. And there a leper came to him. And they come unto him, bringing one sick of palsy.*" Yes, yes. "*Come forth, and he that was dead came forth.*" Dead, touch the dead. Yes, yes. I slapped him with my open hand and then I kissed my fingers.

"Please let me go. Why are you doing this to me?"

"Because you are weak and ugly and dirty."

Defeated, he stood before me. I hated him because he would not resist me. I loved him because he was my victim. I slapped him again. He put a freckled, chubby hand against his cheek.

"Please don't," he pleaded.

"Are you married? Answer me."

"Yes."

"Does your wife know about this ritual?"

"Let me go."

"Does your wife know about this ritual?"

"No, she knows nothing about me, she hates me."

"Ah. Why does she hate you? Has she ever told you she hates you?"

"No, but I know she does."

"How do you know?"

He did not answer. His whole face softened like a papier-mâché mask in water. There were tears in his eyes and his twisted lip trembled.

"How do you know? Answer me."

"Look at me, look at me!" he shouted in a high strained voice, lunging at me and trying to beat my chest with his fists. "I'm ugly, I'm ugly."

I catapulted the palm of my hand hard into his face and he fell backwards. I stood over him and prodded his thigh with my foot.

"You are filthy," I said, and I turned my back on him and walked to the door.

I felt the knob twist in my hand. Someone was trying to enter. I leaned against the door and ordered the baggage clerk to stand up.

"What's going on in there?" called the man from outside.

When he was on his feet, I opened the door and let the angry man in. The temple became a lavatory.

"Must've been stuck," I said to him, happy to flee the lavatory and take the temple home. "I'll see you again," I called to the baggage clerk who was dousing his face in the sink of cold water which I had filled.

He did not answer. Elbows on the edge of the sink, he leaned over the water. Perhaps he could see his reflection on the surface, and he was studying it. Purified and strong, I walked among the people in the station. I said hello to people I did not know and helped an elderly man into a taxi. Humans were my friends; we were all citizens of the lovely grey city which grew around me. Each of us had his secret ceremony; each of us had his secret art. I embraced the noontime throngs with a smile.

XII

You think that I was cruel. You must not think that I was cruel. What is the price we must pay for compassion? What is the deep evil in the martyr's blood that holds him happy in the holy fire? In my history, there was now this minor persecution, a man had been humiliated before another man, but how could this diminish the general love that I generated as I walked through the streets that afternoon? I was in tune with all the traffic of the city. A song that had begun in my heart was being sung suddenly and beautifully by the shoppers and strollers, the motors and horns were declaring it, the buildings vibrating with its rhythm. How sad and beautiful we were, we humans with our suffering and our torturing. I, the torturer, he, the tortured, we, the sufferers. I, suffering in the clear-speared fire of purity, burning, agonized and strangely calm. He, suffering in the dark flames of humiliation and beginning the journey to purity. I, the instrument of his delivery, and he, the instrument of mine. Could it be that the reward of the degraded is to degrade others? Could that be the painful chain toward salvation because I know there is a chain? Humiliation, of course that was it, humiliation. Humiliation was the burden of which I had been relieved. Humiliation, the tapeworm of strength, starving me into lies and cowardice, growing fat in my bowels, a weight dragging me to my knees so that I must crawl. And now, I had purged myself. The technique was not entirely clear to me, but I had purged myself. I could not understand it. I had learned something from my grandfather, no that was not it, rather my grandfather's presence generated some kind of strength. His life, the direct and honorable way he led it, had given me a direction and showed me a road out of humiliation. There was one more humiliation, which I had to inflict on my victim, by which I could completely free myself and which would involve him in a predicament out of which he could begin his journey to purity. But I will come to that in a moment.

I did not go back to work that afternoon, in fact, I did not go back to work at all. For one thing, I was tired of the job and I could not reconcile the tedium of office routine with my new feelings. I had almost one hundred dollars in the bank which was enough to keep my grandfather and I for some time. And most important, I wouldn't have the time if I was to accomplish what I wanted. I wandered that afternoon in the downtown area, window-shopping, eavesdropping on conversations, and delighting in human inventions, indulging myself in this new sense of communication. I was no longer outside the city. Yes, the city did have walls, walls between the pure and the impure, between the weak and the strong, walls of dedication and violence, walls crumbling and repairing themselves, people changing sides as I had done, and people preparing to change as my baggage clerk was doing, and this was the music of life, the music which I loved.

When I returned home that evening, Marylin was already in my room. She was weeping and confused. She ran to me, as I entered, and pressing herself against me, she waited for my encircling arms. I was too strong now. I saw how easy it would be to hold her, to love her, and how weak that would be.

"Hold me," she sobbed, "please, hold me."

I did not hold her. I looked over her shoulder toward my grandfather, who was shaking his head up and down.

"Then it's true, it's true, what your grandfather told me is true? You don't want to marry me? I couldn't believe my ears when he started to tell me."

I wanted to thank my grandfather for telling her, but I thought it would perhaps be too cruel. I would try to be as less as possible through her ordeal.

"Yes, it's true, what my grandfather told you is true."

"I don't understand," she said. "Please, don't say that."

It is interesting to observe that in times of desperation we become extremely, how shall I say, polite. We say, "please" and "thank you" and employ all the amenities.

"I can't marry you, Marylin, I don't love you."

She put her hand softly against my mouth as if to stop the words or to change them.

"No, don't say that, please. What is happening?"

"Nothing is happening. I don't love you. We couldn't live together that way."

She was still leaning against me.

"I think you'd better sit down," I said, leading her to a chair.

She sat down dumbly as if she were obeying an order. She was not even crying any longer.

"You don't love me? You said you loved me." Her voice was flat and pained. "Last night, only last night, on that bed, we undressed, and you loved me, you said you loved me."

"I know," I said. "And I'm sorry I had to deceive you. I have to confess that I lied."

"You have to confess?"

"Yes, that I lied."

"And all these past weeks?"

"I lied, I lied. Oh, Marylin, I'm so sorry to do this to you, I couldn't help myself, I was so weak."

"Somehow," she said, "somehow, I can't believe that everything we experienced here, in this room, everything we felt, all the pledges we made, were lies. I simply can't believe it."

"You must believe it. We must end this now."

I went over to my grandfather who had been watching us in silence.

"Grampa, tell her what you told me, tell her how my face looked."

"Your face?" said Marylin. "What do you mean?"

"He saw us when we made love, he wasn't always asleep."

"Oh, God," she said, "this is unbelievable."

"Tell her, Grampa, please."

He did not understand me at first, but when I made myself clear, he got up and stood beside me in front of her.

Before he began to speak, she said, "I can't bear this. The two of you like impersonal, accusing judges."

"I see his face when he holds you," he said, demonstrating by joining his hands, and making his arms a circle. Marylin turned her eyes away from him. "No, no," he insisted, "you must to watch me." She met his eyes. "Sometimes I see him," he continued, speaking slowly and with difficulty, illustrating with his hands. "Over your neck, I see him, his face full with pain like man with heavy sickness." My grandfather twisted his face in artificial pain. "Like this. Sometimes when you leave little light on, or candle, I see him full with pain." My grandfather leaned close over her face. "Like this."

"No, no, stop it, go away," she shouted at my grandfather. "I don't know what's come over the two of you. Get him away," she pleaded.

I did not move. It was necessary that she heard and understood everything. Suddenly she lifted her foot, pressed it into the old man's stomach and pushed him back, not violently, but firmly. For an instant, I saw his eyes flash with rage, and I feared what was to follow. But he shrugged his shoulders, turned his back, and went out the door, probably to the landlady's room, I supposed.

"Poor Marylin," I said aloud.

"'Poor Marylin,'" she echoed, "how can you say that, how can you humiliate me this way?"

"What way?" I asked belligerently, suddenly weary of the scene.

"How can you speak to me so coldly after all we've been through?"

"Look, Marylin," I said as tenderly as I could, "I don't want to speak to you coldly, and I don't want to be cruel to you, I just don't think it will do us any good to draw it out."

She covered her face with her hands and rocked back and forth. The widows of Ashur are loud in their wail. She seemed swollen and old, older than me, and my house and my city, ancient as woman, ancient as grief, more swollen than the round towers of rotting grain, more swollen than the regiments of drowned floating corpses.

"Can you understand?" I asked her gently. "Can you understand that I love you now? In your grief I love you now."

"Marry me, please, marry me," she wailed. "I'm too old to begin again. I can't begin again."

"Of course, you can begin again, you're still young and you are a beautiful woman." I heard my lips speak the lie and it sickened me. "No," I corrected myself, "you are not young, and you are not beautiful. I must not see you again."

"Oh, God, don't let me hear this."

"There is nothing more to hear. We could say the same things over and over."

"Yes," she said, "yes, we must say the same things over and over. We love each other, I know we do, we could make a life with each other, we could be happy."

She stood up and moved her body against mine. How long will this go on? I wondered. How long will it be before she is gone, before she is walking up the street to her apartment, before she is telling her roommate, before they are weeping, before they are sleeping? Will it be in fifteen minutes, an hour, will she linger until morning? Until then, I must not listen, I must not think, I must not become involved in her grief. Soon, it will be over, it will be completed, we will be separate and free, until then, I must shut her out, I must be an island, a cylinder, a bomb, a silent clock, faceless and chime-less, noiselessly ticking, in my own deep bowel-coiled world. She unbuttoned her blouse and manipulated my hand over her breast, I disowned my hand.

"How can you forget me?" she pleaded.

She made a desperate argument of her body. She plunged her tongue into my mouth. I abandoned my mouth. Goodbye poor mouth, you are un-mourned. She peeled off my ears and half my cheek and made a deep painless gash in my throat. Now she was undressed, and as she removed each piece of clothing, she advertised the flesh under it like a revelation. She was eloquent, but I do not remember what she said. I only thought, *how sad, how sad that she must do this before me, that she has been reduced to this.* The index finger of my left hand held in her hand like a pencil, drowned in liquid for its limp betrayal. Un-mourned.

She manoeuvred me to the bed saying, "How can you forget me?"

She exposed my naked ribs, removing my flesh with my shirt. Freedom at last, I sighed. Why wasn't I allowed to forsake my body temporarily? From where did that commandment come that flashed into my contained world where I was hiding until the ravages had ceased? I will not say God, I would not embarrass you. One day, I shall be able to say God. Let us say it came from memory but stronger, more intense than any memory I had ever known. "*And he shall take a wife in her virginity. A widow, or a divorced woman, or profane, or a harlot, these he shall not take, but he shall take a virgin of his own people to wife.*" I resumed my flesh suddenly like a heavy garment flung onto me by a strong outstretched arm. I cried in ecstasy and agony.

"Let me go!" I cried, wrenching from her arm's circle.

"No, stay with me, please, don't leave me, you just loved me."

She tightened her arms around my neck. I dug my elbows into her ribcage deep and hard.

"Hurt me," she gasped, "I love you."

"Stop it!" I shouted. "Stop talking!"

I struck her face. Her body began to writhe and tremble in an orgy of pain and sexual intoxication.

"Beat me," she pleaded.

I beat her, and I beat her, with my fists and my arms, with my head and knees. Suddenly, the door opened and my grandfather was beside me and he was beating her too and she did not resist, I do not think that she resisted, she urged us to continue, pleading with us not to stop, until the three of us were moving in the same frantic dance, like three items of debris on the same wave of a heaving sea, up and down and up, enemies and comrades in a blind war, murdering and saving by blind manoeuvres, our voices rising and falling to a common rhythm, the clamor and harmony of all men in a total war. When we had exhausted ourselves, we lay apart, breathing together like human clocks. It was all over, the operation, the surgery was completed. After some time, she got up and, like an old woman picking among garbage, recovered her clothes. She was bleeding from one eye. She did not say goodbye. We had performed an eloquent goodbye.

XIII

I have gone too far. I have told you too much. It is a mad story
you say, told by a madman. And truthfully, I am too exhausted at
this moment to care whether you believe it or not. It happened,
that is all, it happened just as Buchenwald happened, and Bergen-
Belsen and Auschwitz, and it will happen again. It will be planned
and it will happen again and we will discover the atrocities, the
outrages and the humiliations, and we will say that it is the plan
of a madman, the idea of a madman; but the madman is ourselves, the violent plans, the cruelties and indignities, they are
all our own and we are not mad, we are crying for purity and love.
It is a long time since all this happened, since I struck or thought
of striking, since I considered violence as a method. Can I smile
now? Can I review this story and sadly smile on the frailties of
man? Can I whisper with sweet remorse, "O World, O Death?"
I can, damn me, I can: because it happened to me; I committed
the little cruelties and violence and I know myself, and I know
that I am not evil; therefore, what is there to do but smile sweetly,

sadly, or weep with some beloved, hold her desperately and tenderly? We are not mad, we are human and we want to love, and someone must forgive us for the paths we take to love, for the paths are many and dark and we are ardent and cruel in our journey, murdering anything in our way, rock, animal, child, or corpse; and someone must forgive us for the rituals we invent to isolate purity, for we want our love to be pure; rituals in which we wash and scrape, and cut and whip, and strip and boil, and mutilate so that the tiny fragment of life we finally hold in our hands is pure and holy, even though around our feet festers the discarded flesh, poisoning the air we breathe; someone must forgive us our failures which are not glorious or worthy enough to record. But now, I must return. I have suspended the story long enough with these reflections.

XIV

It is easy to seduce a woman, especially a wife, especially the wife of a weak and ugly man. That was the final humiliation I had planned, to take his wife, to have her betray him. I set about my task the next morning. I learned my victim's name from the Baggage Master, whom I went to see, with regard to my grandfather's claim.

"Name's Cagely," he said. "Why?"

"Oh, nothing," I replied. "I thought I knew him, he looked familiar."

"Poor old Cagely," he said, "works harder than any three men but somehow doesn't seem to have the goods. Not well liked, you know. Course, he's got a handicap, you might say, with his bad mouth and his funny way of not looking at you when he's speaking to you, not exactly a handicap but it kinda makes it hard to warm up to a fellow like that."

I couldn't bear hearing him discuss this man who had become so important in my life. He had no part of Cagely; Cagely was mine. The name of my man on his lips aroused in me the same resentment I once felt when an acquaintance, in whom I had indiscreetly confided, inquired a week later about the lady in question, using her first name. If he used his name again, I thought I might strike him.

I walked over to Peel Street and waited in front of his rooming house for about an hour, until someone leaving the house gave me the opportunity of entering the vestibule. I checked the nameplates and discovered in which room the Cagelys lived. I remained before the nameplates, pretending to inspect them, prepared to spend all day in that position until she emerged. I do not remember how long I waited. The door finally opened, a woman stepped into the hall, and I left the house. I watched her come down the stairs. I judged her to be older than her husband and taller. She was thin and walked stiffly, her shoulders bent slightly forward. Her lips were thin, and she had not exaggerated their dimensions in applying lipstick: a thin red line between her sharp nose and pointed chin. Perhaps he tore his lip on her face, I speculated humorously. The softness of her eyes contrasted with the razor features. I walked behind her, following her from one store window to another. She did not buy anything. I wondered how I would begin. It was just a matter of getting to talk with her. She turned into the university campus and sat down under a tree. I walked past her and allowed a few minutes to pass. The campus was fairly crowded, people sitting on the grass, eating their lunches and watching spring change the trees. I thought of her, not as a person, certainly not as a bedmate, but as an instrument of reaching the final pain of my victim. When humiliation is private, it is bearable; it is bearable when strangers know of it, but when we are exposed, in all our shame, to those with whom we are intimate, then it is too much to bear. It was this total humiliation that I wanted to inflict on my baggage clerk.

"You seem to have found the best tree and all the others are occupied. May I share it with you?" I asked her.

"Of course," she said.

"It is a lovely day, isn't it?" I said.

There was no point in trying to be subtle.

"Yes, it is."

"It has been a long spring, hasn't it? Still not quite summer."

"We had the same thing three years ago, remember?"

I will not bore you with anymore of this tedious dialogue. We have all had conversations such as this. The words are not important; it's the sexual challenge. She was a woman nearing middle-age, plain-looking, childless, her marriage a failure. She told me these things and many more in our first half-hour of talk, happy to unburden herself to an interested stranger.

"Your husband?" I asked.

"Well, he does his best. I don't suppose I would marry him if I had to do it all over again. I was getting on, all my sisters married, and everyday my mother would say, 'Well, what about you?' After a while I began to panic. I guess I was afraid of being left alone. Gee, I'm sure telling you a lot, aren't I, and we've only met these few minutes."

"That's what talk is for—and strangers. But I don't feel like we're strangers, do you?"

"No," she said, "you're right. It's funny, isn't it?"

"Yes, it is funny, please go on."

"Well, he seemed to be the only one around, so I married him. He's a good man, sometimes I think I might have done better but he's a good man. We all have to make a life for ourselves."

It was only a matter of time before we would be on some bed and I would be praising her ruined body, and she mine, and she would be remembering her hatred for the man who took her for his bride and buried her in a rooming house of a great city. Her dream was so easy to understand. She was old, and her husband was ugly and weak, and her dream was of passion. Her dream was of a stranger who would take her like a child bride, who would understand her love, her passion, her strength, and nourish her, and let her flourish. Her dream was everyone's dream, everyone's secret, a dream of fire and violence, and tenderness, a dream of the heart's discovery and fulfillment. It was easy to the stranger. I bought her lunch and then we went to her room.

"This is where I live," she said. "This is where I have ended."

"You are still a young woman," I said. "I can feel your youth and your vitality. You could begin again. You still have a life ahead of you."

Perhaps she knew the lie as well as I did but this was one afternoon of her life and, to her, the lie was beautiful.

"I feel young," she said, standing before me with her shoulders pulled backwards, in an attempt to show off her small breasts.

"I want to have children. I want to teach children."

Then we made love. Fortunately, I remember nothing. I tried to be skillful. Yes, I do remember something. I remember her closed eyes and her open mouth and a shell on the mantle with NIAGARA FALLS written on it.

"You are my lover," she said naively. "I have always wanted a lover."

This was not her betrayal. The naked body, the trembling, the climax, these had nothing to do with betrayal. The betrayal began in the aftermath of her passion. We had been lying in silence.

"He never made love to me like that," she said. "He wouldn't know how. I mean, he hasn't got any imagination, you know what I mean. When I think of all these years and he tried, mind you, he tried. But I never felt anything for him. I never felt anything for his body. I've wanted this for so long. He doesn't understand me. I never expected him to understand me, but I never knew it would be so hard. It's terrible to say this, I know, the man tries so hard, he's not smart but he always made a living, but I can't forgive him, I feel like he's ruined my life, like he's taken everything out of me. Isn't that a terrible thing to say?"

"I understand," I said, stroking her coarse hair. "I understand everything."

I left her after we had agreed to meet the following day.

On the second day, she said, "I'm so happy I don't know what to say. I'd always dreamed I'd meet someone like you, I can hardly believe the things you tell me. Sometimes, I think there must be someone else in the room who you're speaking to, but I look around and it's only you and me. Can it be possible that you really want me? It's a wonderful thing to feel like a woman; it's like being born again. I wonder what he'd say if he knew, if he knew that I had a lover, me, who he did a favor by marrying."

On the third day, she said, "Last night, I told him that I had a lover. I had to tell him, I couldn't bear it any longer. All he said was, 'You got a lover?' He didn't believe me, he couldn't believe me. I yelled at him, 'I have a lover, I have a lover!' He couldn't say anything. I never told you this but he's ugly, that's the only word for it. I told him I hated him for what he'd done to me. All he did was shake his head up and down like a fool."

On the fourth day, she said, "I hate him. I don't think I could stand it if he tried to kiss me. I'd die. You've never seen him, he's got a lip that looks like a sore. He must've made me kiss it a thousand times. No, I shouldn't tell you that, you won't want to kiss me. How can you love me? I'm so old."

I kissed her. I encouraged her revenge. He had ravaged her. He had defiled her. I had given her a logic for her hatred, I was no longer important to her. It is not rare for a woman to despise a man who has taken her youth and her innocence, but most women remember that the rape was attended by pledges and romance and music. There had been no romance for her, no music, and the pledges were chains. He had rescued her from spinsterhood, and she could never forgive him for that; rescued her with a weak freckled body and a torn lip and a dull mind. I had broken the dam of her hatred and the flood would consume everything.

On the fifth day, she said, "He won't believe me, he still can't believe me. He can't believe there is anyone who loves me like I say you do. Please, don't mind me telling him. I have to tell him. Last night, I wouldn't get into bed with him. I couldn't stand lying beside him. He tried to pull me, and I hit him. I said, 'Look at yourself, see what you are, think anyone would want to sleep with you?' He took hold of my arm and begged me. He was excited, sexually I mean, hopping around like a dog in heat. He tried to touch me here and I hit him again. I know I was cruel, but you can't blame me after what he's done to me. Later, I said to him, 'We're strangers, just remember that we're strangers.' I think he was crying. That's one thing I can't stand, a man crying, it turns my stomach. And then, do you know what I saw? I'm almost embarrassed to tell you. There was a little light in the room, and I saw the blankets moving up and down. He was, well, you know, he was abusing himself right there with me in the room. I crept up and pulled the blankets right off of him. 'What a pig you are,' I told him. He just curled up in a ball with his face in the pillow and cried like a baby. 'You haven't got a lover,' he sobs, 'please, say you haven't got a lover.' It's really bothering him. Then I lied to him, I don't know why, just to make him suffer, like I did. I told him that I'd always had a lover, that you weren't the first, that there was always someone else from the very beginning, even when we were first married. Then he started hitting his own head with his hand and then he tried to crawl all over me. It was a disgusting performance, but it didn't surprise me."

XV

And so, for the next few days, she continued to torture him, to revenge herself on him. I was with him in his suffering, sustaining him, encouraging him to find his way to cleanliness through total humiliation. I often went to the station to observe him, to see if I could detect traces of the struggle on his face. He seemed unmoved, but I knew what was raging in his mind and heart. I knew the shame, I knew the humiliation, I had felt it, it had raged within me. An old shame, an old guilt, an old humiliation, older than my body and his body, older than words and worlds, older than God himself. The creation was the beginning of shame, the birth of God, the birth of the first star, the violence of creation, the vicious stab into nothingness that brought forth rock and water and flesh; before the stab, the motion of the stab began the shame; the idea of the stab brought forth shame. Shame turned the space into air and the light into rock. Sometimes, I would think a prayer to myself. A prayer full of those paradoxes which have meaning only to the obsessed. A prayer, of old words and old ambiguities, which meant nothing but the music, the rhythm of dedication and purity. And I would sometimes sway as I spoke it, hidden behind my pillar, the low steel counter like an altar, polished and washed and clean, my victim rushing like a stricken man between the altar and the mysterious and complicated racks of leather bags. And in each bag was a life, a soul, and the bodies lined up waiting for him to return their souls, and he returned them at my bidding, suffering under the weight of each one, struggling to heave it onto the altar, and they paid him with golden tickets. Suffer my little priest, my little victim, suffer my misery, my distress, my sorrow. Learn betrayal so that you may not betray. Learn shame, remember humiliation, be diligent in your recollection of guilt. Wash your blood in the clean waters of pain, make your flesh a filter for the river of anguish, your bones a channel for the flood of bitterness. I am with you, you are beside my right hand, you embrace me, but you cannot touch me, I have gone before you. Understand contamination so you may be pure, violence so you may be peaceful. Be pure with me; smother in dung so you might breathe freely. How beautifully he performed his ritual, my ritual, his flesh bathed in milk, his deformed lip, a mark upon his face, lest anyone finding him should kill him, wandering to-and-fro between the altar and the racks, the precious weight of life in his arms.

Hocus-pocus. I know. I will not try and justify these days, days when I moved in an absurd dream of purity, speaking phony slogans like a fake mystic, committing cruelty and adultery in the home of a stranger. I will not try and justify these days. I would need a different vocabulary and a different listener, and I do not want a different vocabulary or a different listener. I want you more than anything, I want you. I do not want you to turn away. I do not want you to turn away. I do not want you to lower your eyelids which shut me out like fragile unassailable gates. I do not want you to adjust the sheets about your body as if you were preparing for a long sleep and turn and plunge slowly into those deep caves where I cannot follow. Ah, now, you are sleeping, and I am totally excluded. Now, I will say that I love you, that I have always loved you, that I have stood beside your sleeping body so many times and told you so many times that I have loved you so long. I cannot disagree on anything you may say about these days. Remember only one thing: they were ordered and happy. In all their foolish hocus-pocus, they had more meaning than any other period of my life. I don't suppose that ever again will I have that feeling of integration, dedication, and mission, the delicious surrender of my life to a higher cause. Even now, as I remember this period, I recall it as a glorious march among passionate men. I do not wish to recall it too intimately. I want always to be reminded of it but not in detail, but rather like a gold blur somewhere in my history. Now, there remains for me only to tell you of the termination of this episode of my life. I am surprised to have come this far without having revealed more of myself to you. I feel that I have hardly spoken, that we are still strangers. I told you that Mrs. Cagely was more interested in revenging herself on her poor husband than in whatever love there happened to be between us. I was as much an instrument of hers as she was of mine. Of course, this is often the case among lovers, and it was exactly as I had planned it. I was waiting for the day when she would insist on showing me to her husband, and on that day his humiliation would be complete.

"Can you believe it?" she said to me, "He won't let himself believe that I have a lover. He tries to make a joke of it. I feel like his not believing it somehow makes our love little less than it is."

It was amazing how we could discuss "our love." Neither of us believed in it or wanted it and yet the phrase crept into our vocabulary because of its convenience and we used it as a slogan for our individual missions. We talked about our victim for hours before and after and during our lovemaking. I used his name and his ugliness to arouse her and she told me stories of his impotence to arouse me. We both panted as we spoke of his milky freckled skin, his thin limbs, and his mutilated mouth, we grunted to examples of his stupidity and climaxed in curses on his pathetic hopeless life. We decided that we would confront him with "our love" the following afternoon.

"Do you think he will become violent?" I asked her.

"Him, violent? Don't make me laugh. He'll probably just break down and cry."

Her pointed face shone dully like a razor in the shadowy room. She moved out of my embrace and lay on her back facing the ceiling, her hands behind her head.

"I just can't wait," she said, "to see his face."

"He'll lick his lips," I said.

"He'll try and make a joke," she said.

"Maybe he'll turn and run," I said.

"Where could he run to?" she said.

"The room will be dark," I said. "He won't see us at first."

"He won't believe it, until he sees it," she said.

"Let's stay in bed when he comes," I said. "Let's not get dressed."

"Yes, yes," she said. "That's the only way he'll believe it. And after he sees us and we talk to him, I want you to leave. I want to be with him alone, do you understand?"

"Of course, I understand."

I kissed her small dried breasts.

"Of course, I understand," I told her.

"Will you want to see me again?" I asked her, already know-ing the answer.

"I don't think so," she said. "I like you very much, but there's not much further we could go."

"You're right," I said, with genuine tenderness, "we've both done what we wanted." She nodded her head.

"I suppose you'll find someone else," she said. "You're the kind of man who needs a woman."

"I suppose," I said.

XVI

That evening as I walked home, I was aware that a chapter of my life was drawing to an end. I did not know what I would do after the affair with the baggage clerk was over and I did not care. I only knew that I was in the midst of some test, some important ritual, and that I was nearing the end of my term as neophyte. Spring was definitely on the city. There seemed to be people at every corner, just lingering. Young men, with greased hair and open shirts, stood against walls and plotted fantastic orgies with every passing female. Old men clustered around public benches and set up new governments. The buds and the fertile smell, which even managed to penetrate the downtown area, seemed to affirm my new life of purity. The landlady and my grandfather were sitting on the balcony, enjoying the mildness. I did not resent her perverse attachment to my grandfather as long as he did not. Who was to say who was using who? Of late, she had become his constant companion, and since my own mind was so preoccupied with my ritual so that I was bad company for anyone, I appreciated her attention to the old man.

"It's your grandson," she said to him, as I climbed the stairs.

As usual, he did not recognize me until I stood before him.

"Ah, hello, my darling."

"You never call me that," said the landlady to him, but he ignored her.

Then she said to me, "They called you from the office again. They want you to fill out some papers or something. I told them you'd be in sometime."

"That was the correct thing to tell them." I would be in sometime. Soon I would have to make some money but not for a while, at least not until after tomorrow. "And how have you been, Grampa?"

"Good, good. How should I have been? An old man is good anywhere."

The landlady laughed and stroked his hair. "Listen to him," she said, "and with all the comforts of home." She pinched his cheek. He caught her hand and flung it against the arm of the chair. It hurt her, but she was not sure whether he had done it in anger or in jest. My grandfather laughed as if someone had just told a joke and the landlady decided to laugh also.

"Isn't he the fierce one?" she said, through a weak laugh.

"Yah, fierce, fierce," he said, and slapped her thigh.

"I'll leave you two to fight it out," I said, entering the house.

"I'll give him supper," she called after me.

I did not feel like eating. This day, like the others, was of such an emotional intensity that I was very tired. I removed my shoes and my jacket, lay down on my bed and was soon asleep.

It was the middle of the night when my grandfather awakened me. I got up and turned on the light. He was very excited, breathing heavily. He motioned with his cane toward the hall.

"Come, come," he said.

I followed him down the hall to the landlady's room. Her door was open. The scene that greeted me looked like the cover of a pulp detective novel. A lamp on the dresser washed the room in a rusty light. An elaborate crucifix, casting a shadow of spikes, hung above the iron bed. On the dresser, on a mirrored plate, rose a glass fortress of perfume and medicine bottles. Into the frame of the mirror were wedged snapshots and religious pictures. Wallpaper of huge roses in columns hung loosely from a grape cluster moulding. The room was the distillery of that particular odor the landlady always exuded. She was flung diagonally across her bed, face-down, naked, one arm tangled in sheets, the other hanging limply over the side of the bed. She was not unconscious, she was sobbing. There were red welts across her back and buttocks. Actually, I could make out the design of my grandfather's carved cane in the red raised bruises. My grandfather hopped around the bed, brandishing his cane, looking toward me for approval. It was the first time since I had known him that I considered the possibility that he was insane. He made a little skip and brought the cane down on her shoulders. She made no effort to defend herself. She gave out a pathetic moan, trembled and resumed her sobbing. My grandfather danced to my side and handed me the cane, inviting me to strike her.

"Come, come," he urged pulling my arm toward the bed. "I help you with Marylin, remember?"

Stunned, I took the cane from him. He pulled her hair with both hands and spit at her head. This was violence which had no logic, no purpose. Its aim was only the infliction of pain on another human being. He was mad, certainly, he was mad.

"Come, come," he beckoned, pounding her buttocks like a drum.

The room was suddenly dirty, full of contamination. My grandfather hovered over the woman, thumping, pinching, pulling as if she were a work of art of his own creation which he now despised and wished to mutilate. She lay in the orange light, like an exhumed corpse, her hair tangled, and her body bruised, trembling vaguely under his blows, sobbing and choking on her saliva. Purposeless violence. I lunged toward him and pinned his arms down to his side.

"What, what?" he demanded.

He squirmed out of my grasp and kicked me in the groin. I threw my fist into his enraged face and then into his stomach. He fell to the floor gasping.

"Keep it down in there," called a roomer from across the hall.

My grandfather was hurt, his mouth covered with blood. He was muttering something in a foreign tongue. I could not bear the orange light. I tore the lampshade off and exposed the naked bulb. I disentangled the sheet from her arm and covered her body with it. My grandfather clawed at my ankle as I passed him. I went to the bathroom and soaked a towel in cold water. I washed her shoulders and her face. She tried to lie on her back, but she could not.

"Thank you," she said weakly.

I carried my grandfather back to my room and adjusted him on my bed. I cleaned his face with a shirt someone had flung in the corner.

"My darling," he said, "you must not to hit your grandfather. I am an old man. I swimmed lake once. I can no more. I was only man to swim lake. Everyone try to beat me. I alone swim lake."

He tried to move his arms in a swimming motion. The struggle had exhausted him, and he fell asleep. I moved between the two rooms the rest of the night, bringing the landlady water and a little hot soup, watching over my grandfather, thinking of nothing but making the two old bodies comfortable. Morning came, and the landlady was still sleeping. I left some cold cereal and a glass of milk beside her bed. My grandfather greeted me warmly, apparently having forgotten about the preceding evening. I did not remind him. I resolved to watch him more closely in the future. I would have more time to spend with him after I had completed the episode with my baggage clerk. My baggage clerk, my victim, I had almost forgotten about the importance of the day. This was the day of confrontation, of resolution. The doorbell rang. It rang a second time, before I realized that the landlady was in no condition to answer it. Another roomer had answered it by the time I got there. There were four people standing in the vestibule, three men and a woman. One was a policeman. I was not surprised. I did not know why a policeman had come, but I was not surprised. One of the other men spoke my name like a question.

"Yes," I said, "will you come in?"

The four entered my room.

"That's him," cried one of them, "and he ran to my grandfather's bed. This is him," he said, "this is my grandfather."

"What, what?" spoke my grandfather startled.

"I don't understand," I said.

The man who had asked me my name said, "I'm Detective Forret. I think we've got a little surprise for you."

"Yes," said the woman, "just a little surprise."

"Let the detective tell him, dear," said the man who was sitting beside my grandfather. "He won't give us any trouble."

"I'm sure he won't," the woman said bitterly, "he's probably anxious to get rid of him."

"What are you talking about," I demanded.

"You see," said Forret, "a mistake has been made. This man," he said, pointing to my grandfather, "this man, whom you believe to be your grandfather, is not your grandfather at all, he is this gentleman's grandfather."

"This is absurd," I said.

"I agree," said the woman, "you keep the old boy and let's forget this ever happened."

Her husband stood up and shouted at her, "I forbid you to talk about my father's father in that manner! It will be a great honor to have him in our house."

"A great honor, I'm sure," she said, "another mouth to feed, more shirts to wash, another setting at the table, a great honor."

"Well, folks, that's something you'll have to settle among yourselves. I've got something to explain to this gentleman here."

"Please do," I said. "I don't know what any of you are talking about."

"It's just as I said," Forret continued, "he isn't your grandfather. The party that phoned you from New York made a mistake. There were just dialing one number after another until they found his family. You happen to have the same name and so they tried you too. If you had said no, you weren't his grandson, they would have eventually got to this gentleman here and everything would have been all right. Why did you say you were his grandson, anyway? The record shows that your grandfather died some years ago."

"My father's name was Frederik," I said blankly.

"It's a big world," said the husband arrogantly, "my father's name was Frederik too; that's hardly the point."

"I don't believe it," I said desperately, "you have to prove it to me."

The husband produced a cardboard envelope from his inside pocket and handed it to me. It contained letters and photographs, the accumulation of a family's history. I sat down and laid them out on the table before me. The evidence was overwhelming. There were photographs of my grandfather as a young man and in family groups, none of the members of which I could recognize. The husband looked over my shoulder.

"That's my father," he said, pointing to a boy standing beside my grandfather. "And there's the two of them at our wedding."

"Black day that it was," interjected his wife.

I looked over at my grandfather who was lying with his face turned to the wall, oblivious to everything that was going on. The four strangers hovered above me.

"I guess you're convinced now," said Forret.

"No, I'm not convinced!" I shouted, "I'm not convinced at all!"

"This is ridiculous," the husband said, appealing to the detective. "Isn't this the reason we brought the constable along?"

"We're all nice and legal," said Forret, "but let's try and take things easy."

"What about the cart and the animals?" I shouted suddenly.

"What do you mean?" asked Forret.

"Oh, he told you about that, did he?" said the husband in a bored voice. "That's an old story famous in our family. As a young man, my father collected in his new cart, a gift from his father if I remember the tale, all the dogs and cats in the village and sent the whole mess down to the bottom of the lake."

"Just the sort of thing he'd do," said his wife.

Suddenly, I felt lonely, suddenly, I was cast out of the city. *You are alone, you are alone*, a shrill silent voice throbbed in the soft coils of my mind. *You are alone now, and you have always been alone.*

"Please, don't go," I said politely to the strangers. "I'll make some coffee."

"I'm afraid we don't have the time. Thanks just the same." The husband shook his head and laughed.

They helped my grandfather out of the bed and assisted him with his jacket. He offered no resistance. I don't think he quite understood what was happening. The voice in my mind proclaimed my loneliness over and over like a passionate promise of an oracle. *Now you have no one, now you have nothing.*

I gave myself over to panic.

"Please, don't take him!"

None of them paid any attention.

"I think he's got everything," said the husband.

"Grampa!" I shouted in the old man's face. "They're taking you away from me!"

I stepped in front of the door to prevent their exit. With a growl, he collected saliva in his mouth and spit at me. "My darling," he said, "you must not to hit an old man." Then he turned to the husband and said, "Last night he beat me."

"Lovely people we're getting to know," said the wife.

"Let's all take it easy," said Forret.

"You can't take him," I pleaded, "you can't take him. I love him. He's my grandfather. I won't let you. You won't know how to handle him. He's dangerous. Do you know there's a woman down the hall whom he almost beat to death last night?" Then I appealed to the policeman. "And the very first day in the city, he struck a policeman with his cane, this cane. And then he took it to the woman. And he threw excrement, his own excrement, in the landlady's face."

"Charming," said the woman, "just charming."

"I think we've had enough of this, Mr. Forret," said the husband.

Forret nodded to the policeman, who grabbed my arm and pushed me away from the door. I spit in his face.

"Did you see that, sir?" he said. "Did you see that?"

"Better be careful," said Mr. Forret.

"Better be careful," said the husband.

The five of them moved into the vestibule and out onto the balcony. I ran after them. The policeman was the last to leave the vestibule and I crashed into his chest. He quickly glanced behind him to see if any of the others were watching. They were busy descending the steps with my grandfather, helping him at every stair. He stiffened his open hand and brought the edge down between my neck and shoulder. I fell to the floor and with his foot he shoved me back a few feet, so I could not be seen by the others. Then he turned and left.

"You won't keep him," I sobbed after them. "He'll kill all of you. He's a murderer. He's dying. He's mine. He's mine!"

XVII

I lay on the floor for some time, my cheek against the sobering cold tile. The tiles were rust-colored and each one was surrounded by a moat of cement. Tiles were smooth; cement was rough. There was a stack of muddy rubbers and galoshes in one corner, huddling together like blind subterranean animals. An umbrella rose from their midst like a black, poisonous tree. Now the tiles were flat unplanted fields watered by an intricate irrigation system. Now they were squares of a chessboard and I plotted a checkmate with an invisible regiment. Now the tiles were islands in a calm cement ocean, each one close to the other, very close but never, never touching. Somewhere, in the midst of my fantasy, a car sped away bearing my grandfather and his new victims. His new victims: a husband and his dissatisfied wife. And then, someone would take him to another house and after that another and another. I saw him moving through all the buildings of the city, cane in hand, teaching everyone he passed a dangerous, beautiful ritual of violence. A ritual which he himself abused. The beating of the landlady—that was beyond the ritual. I saw him moving through families and churches and courts, tempting every man with a new life and a new dedication. Or had he really had any effect on my life? Was I attributing to him some influence which he had never had? Wasn't violence taught eloquently enough in this city, in the forest, in the changing sky? I was alone now, I was alone. My room would be as empty as my life. *Purity, dedication:* I spoke the words over and over. They meant nothing. I felt like the victim of a stupid joke. What nonsense I had let myself believe. What utter nonsense. I am so lonely, I said to my untouching islands, fixed in their stone sea and I tried to pry out two tiles so that I could lay them together. My fingers were bleeding when I finally stood up. I felt a deep pain in my shoulder. I shut the incident out of my mind. I did not wish to review that farcical scene which had just been acted in my room. That's what it had been, a farce, complete with exhumed family papers and mistaken identities. But this cynical reflection did not assuage the pain in my shoulder or my finger, or the deep pain in my mind which embraced the physical pain like a poor brother and made it its own.

I went into my room which seemed now like an open plain and I could not bear its vastness. The beds were huge, barren promontories and the ceiling an impossible sky. The walls had dissolved onto a colorless desert. In the street, the people were busy ghosts walking in twos and threes between the dark, soft brick. Nothing was concrete but the pain and the growing panic of loneliness. The face of one building contrasted with the blurred city. I climbed the stairs and found my way to her door. I remember the doorbell because it was hard against my injured finger.

"You're early," said Mrs. Cagely. "What's the matter with you? You look like you got hit by a cyclone."

I said nothing. I lay on the bed and, for the first time, surveyed the room. It was green, in fact it was the same green of the baggage room where her husband worked. A white plaster moulding supported a ceiling which was bent down the middle like a piece of cardboard. A vein of new plaster traced out the bend. An elaborate iron gas fireplace wound itself like a metal digestive system below the mantle. On the mantle, there was a small bank calendar, a wedding photograph, and the souvenir shell which had caught my attention the first afternoon I made love to her. On each of the four walls was a large print of a northland scene. He had probably got them from the Railroad. There was nothing feminine in the room, no perfume bottles or cosmetics or silk straps. There was no trace of any individual expression of her own life. Nor of his, for that matter. Not a pipe or magazine or cufflink. The top of the dresser was bare except for a soiled lace doily. It might have been the waiting room in some starving dentist's office. I could not think of anything a woman could do here. There was no trace of food. She sat down on the bed beside me and took my hand.

"Your fingers are all bruised," she said. "What have you been doing?"

The warmth of her hand argued for safety and I kissed the human flesh. I wanted her to stay beside me. She was the only one I knew in the city.

"I'll undress," she said.

She took off each piece of clothing, carefully folded it, and put in a drawer of the dresser. I imagined her body beside mine and longed for it.

"Here, let me help you with your necktie. What happened to your shoulder?"

"I fell—no, no, it doesn't matter. Please lie here. I want you beside me."

She got into bed beside me, yawned and stretched.

"This is the day," she said. "This is the day I've waited for a long, long, time. Wait, let me pull down the blinds."

"Please, don't get out of bed."

"What's the matter with you today? You're like a little boy. We can't do this in broad daylight."

"Hurry, please."

"All right," she laughed. "I'll hurry."

She covered herself with the bedspread and darkened the room.

"Now that didn't take too long, did it?" she said, snuggling beside me. "It gets dark late now. There will be just enough light for my husband to see the both of us. Then we'll see whether he believes me or not."

"Please, don't let him come, please, don't let him come," I prayed desperately to myself.

"I can just see him standing there now, licking his lip," she said. "He'll cry, that's all, would you like to bet he just breaks down and cries? That'll really be something to see."

As she spoke, she began to caress me, her motions becoming more passionate as the description of her distressed husband became more eloquent.

"He'll be down on his hands and knees. I know what he's like when he gets excited. Right down on his hands and knees."

"We can't let this happen," I wanted to tell her. "We can't let this happen. It's all been a mistake. We have no right to do this to him." But I could not tell her these things. I could not speak. I was too frightened that she would stop caressing me, that she would get up from the bed and pull down all the blinds of the city, that she would leave me alone. I did not speak as she made love to me and I do not think she cared. She used my body like a string of religious beads, grasping this limb, stroking this part, telling her revenge over and over, and she did not notice me shudder and relax in the midst of her rosary.

"Now we will just lie here," she said, "and wait for him."

I tried to gather her in my arms, but her body was stiff and angular. I wished that she would rub my shoulder, but she did not. "Be grateful to be beside a human," I told myself. There are millions lying alone. Landlady, poor landlady, she was lying alone. And as I sank into sleep, I saw multitudes of isolated sleepers, turning, turning, a breath from each other, but never, never touching.

"That's right," she said, drawing me closer. "You go to sleep in the meantime."

I slept on her small breast dreaming not of humans but of stars, galaxies and moons slowly whirling in the firmament.

"I think I hear him," she said, sitting up.

We listened as the front door closed and footsteps drew towards us down the hall.

"It's him," she whispered nervously. "I recognize his walk." She flung away the bedclothes. "I don't want him to miss anything," she said.

The door opened and closed, a shaft of light striking our bodies for an instant. I knew the small silhouette. The room was quite dark. He could not see our faces.

"Hello," she said. "Why don't you turn on the light?"

Something, which was not quite a word, escaped from his mouth.

"Why don't you come a little closer?" she taunted. Automatically, he stepped toward the bed. My fear and his fear, my shame and his shame surged through the room like a flood. "I suppose you'd like to meet my friend. He's the one I told you about. Remember?" The cruelty in her voice was unbelievable.

I did not want him to see me. I buried my face in her belly and encircled her waist with my arms. My nakedness burned me. "What are you doing?" she said, surprised.

"I love you," I mumbled into her flesh. "Cover me, please, cover me."

She was confused. With both her hands, she tried to pry my head from her stomach.

"He mustn't see me, he mustn't see me," I swore.

I tightened the circle of my arms and dug my head deeper.

"You're ruining everything," she gasped. "You're hurting me."

"I love you," I repeated over and over. "Please, don't leave me alone!"

Now I was on my knees, the weight of my back and shoulders thrust down into her stomach, my arms trembling with the pressure of their hold.

"My ribs," she cried in pain, her voice ending in a breathless cough.

She clawed my neck with her fingernails, and I felt her stomach convulse under my forehead. She flung her arms back and wretched frantically making for the edge of the bed.

"I love you. Don't leave me. I love you!"

I smelled the sickening fluid. My knee slid in it. She was choking and kicking her legs up and down, like a sprinting swimmer. *We are going down*, I thought. *We are all going down. This is the end. It is finished. We are drowning for the very last time and I am happy to be struggling out my last breath, naked and burning on this poisonous bed in the half-dark waiting room of death.*

"Help!" she wheezed. "Help me!"

I felt his hands dig into my shoulders, prying me away. I winced as he kneaded the morning wound. He gouged his fingers in my eyes and mouth and pulled my head back.

"Don't look at me," I pleaded. "You know me." But it did not matter for we were descending, the three of us, slowly and calmly though we struggled, the flames of our bodies extinguished, descending through thick water and soft moving weeds into the gentle rolling mud.

"It's you!" he said, disbelieving his eyes. "It's you, it can't be you!"

"Kill him!" she shrieked, scratching my face.

"Yes, it's me," I whispered to myself with a little humor. "Come join us comrade. We are sinking, sinking to rest finally and it has been a long, long fall." He threw himself upon me, smashing my head and shoulders with his fists and elbows.

"You've made my life miserable!"

I covered my face with my arms, but I did not move as they beat me. Soon they stopped. My shoulder was aching painfully. They would have to help me dress. She was in his arms and he was wiping her mouth with a handkerchief.

"Don't cry, don't cry," he told her.

"Get him out of here," she sobbed. "I don't ever want to see him again. I hate him. I hate him."

"I don't know who you are, mister, or why you've done this to us, but you better get the hell out of here, before I call the police."

"Where do you keep your dirty pictures?" I asked him, for no reason at all. "Does your wife know what you do in the toilet?" I did not ask the questions to embarrass him, but to hear myself, how utterly absurd they were. I was glad I had spoken them. They were utterly meaningless. He struck my mouth.

"Get out of here. Get out of here right now."

"You'll have to help me dress," I said, noting the taste of blood on my tongue. "My shoulder is in pretty bad shape." With some difficulty, I got up from the bed. I switched on the light. He drew the bedspread over her. I looked at my clothes folded on a chair. I looked under the chair and then under the bed. The bed smelled foully. "I can't seem to find my underwear," I announced.

"Top drawer," muttered Mrs. Cagely, and she added by way of explaining herself, "I hate to see things lying around."

I put on my clothes. He helped me with my shirt. I inspected the wedding picture and the shell. The shell was coated with brown varnish. What a strange old-fashioned fireplace it was. I inquired whether it still worked but received no answer. "I'm sorry things didn't work out," I said.

She looked away in disgust. He licked his lip which, at that moment, did not seem extraordinary. I took no pleasure in his ugliness. I left them comforting each other and walked down into the street. There was still light left in the day. Soft and grey, the buildings rose around me like huge tongueless guardians. I was careful not to step in the cracks of the sidewalk. This was difficult to do without breaking my pace. No one greeted me or watched me as I passed. I was anonymous. The automobiles were beginning to switch on their lights. Perhaps Marylin would be at my room. Suddenly, I wanted her to hold, to tell my freedom to. I remembered her every movement, the motion of her buttocks when she walked, the direction of every tiny earthquake when she heaved her chest, the way her thighs spread like lava when she sat down, the sudden coil her stomach made before the brink of orgasm, each orchard of hair, blonde and black, the path of pores on the nose, the chart of vessels in her eyes, the special wound color of her lips. She was not waiting for me when I reached my room. I looked forward to some days of privacy. I passed the landlady's room. She was moaning softly. I decided to warm her some soup.

SHORT
STORIES

Saint Jig

"Well, what did you do next?"

Henry asked the question with sympathy. He knew his friend was suffering.

"I bought her a drink. It was no use."

"What kind of drink?"

"Vodka and coke, like you told me. I even had one myself. What a lousy concoction."

Jig made a face.

"And then?"

"Then I bought her another one, and after that, another one. Cost me eight bucks for liquor in the end and that's not counting the taxi and the movie. And what do I get for all that? Nothing, sweet old goose egg, nothing."

"Jig, are you sure you did everything like I told you? Get enough vodka into Patsy and anyone in pants can make the scene with her."

Henry immediately regretted what he had said when he saw his roommate lower his eyes. Jig was so damn sensitive. Patsy was the fourth girl he had fixed him up with. All of them had been fair-looking girls, not too choosy, who viewed bed-going like any other simple recreation, bowling or canasta, and didn't fuss too much about who was their partner, as long as they had one. Very easy targets, especially Patsy, but Jig hadn't scored once. And Jig was a good-looking kid. So what if his left hand was slightly deformed? That didn't make a guy a cripple.

"Yes," Jig replied wearily, "I did everything exactly like you told me. I took her to a horror picture like you told me. She squirmed and tittered all through the stupid thing."

"And what did you do? Did you move in?"

"I didn't do a damn thing. I couldn't. The way it worked out, she was sitting on my left side."

Jig clenched his good fist and banged his kneecap three or four times.

"Oh! Sorry."

"Don't be sorry, Hen. You've been a real friend to me, fixing me up and all that. I just can't seem to come through. Sometimes, I feel that they want it, but then I start thinking about my hand and I figure they wouldn't want something like that travelling all over their bodies. Other times, they just don't appeal to me and I wonder what the hell I'm doing there with them." He added bitterly, "I'll probably die a virgin."

Henry thought back to his first experience. He didn't remember her face. She had been a pro at the Forty-Two Club. Jig was staring down at his left hand. Suddenly he waved his withered fingers in front of Henry's face and burst out, "I ask you, Henry, what broad would want this crawling over her thigh?"

"For Christ's sake, forget about the hand." He tried to speak gently because he genuinely wanted to help this poor guy who didn't know what to do when he got into a room with a woman. "Look, Jig, nobody cares about that hand of yours. You're the only one it bothers, and you talk like you're some kind of freak. Nobody gives a damn about your hand."

"Patsy did."

"What do you mean?"

"Well, I took her home and I was making small talk with her outside her apartment door, like you told me to do. She hadn't noticed my hand; I'd kept it in my pocket most of the time. After a while, we got to making out a little and I was working on her neck like you told me. She was breathing pretty hard, and I figured that finally I had it made and that she was going to invite me inside like you said she always does. Then it happened." Jig got up and stood beside his desk, flipping the pages of a book.

"What happened?"

Jig spoke quickly, unwilling to dwell on the scene. "She took my hand, my left hand, and put it on her breast. I tried with all my might, but I couldn't hold it there. It slipped off. She put it up there again and the same thing happened. Then she stepped back and gave me a really dirty look. 'Whatsamatta,' she said, 'aren't ya interested?'"

Henry chuckled. "What did you say then? That could have been a great opening."

"I didn't say anything. I ran."

"You what?"

"I ran. Down the stairs into the street and then for a block or two. All a big joke to a Casanova like yourself, I suppose."

Henry hated himself for having chuckled. "Sorry, Jig. Must have been pretty rough."

"And stop apologizing all over the place!"

There was a moment or two of silence as they looked at each other.

"Listen Jig, I know I've suggested this to you before and that you haven't liked it, but you ought to think of it seriously. Why don't you go down to the Forty-Two Club, that's where I got my first—"

"I'm not going to pay for it," Jig interrupted him firmly. "I'm not going to pay for it."

"I paid for it and I managed to survive. I'll clue you in on all the details."

"It's different for me, Hen, can't you understand? You can have any girl you want, anytime. I've seen how women act with you. I'm cherry and I admit I'm pretty desperate, but I've got to believe that the girl wants it because of me with my hand and all, and not a lousy ten buck bill."

"Jig, you poor bastard, you're overestimating the whole thing. Every girl is a pro; every girl has her price. If it's not ten bucks, then it's a wedding ring."

"Well, I'd rather give a wedding ring. Then at least you're getting something that belongs to you, that every guy who happens to have a fat wallet can't have."

"Boy, have you got a lot to learn. After you've had your first piece, you'll look at it differently, believe me. You'll wonder what you got so concerned about. Anyway, it's too late now to argue with you. Let's sack."

"I just want to say one more thing, Hen. I appreciate all you've done for me, don't think I don't, but those girls, Patsy and the rest, I don't think they're my type. Horny as I am, I can't seem to really get excited over them. Even if I could have got into Patsy's apartment, I don't know if I could have gone through with it."

"Listen, Jig, when a broad's lying beside you in the dark and she's panting, and her legs start twining around yours, you can go through with it all right."

"Maybe you can, Henry."

Henry laughed. "Believe me, Jig, anybody can. Goodnight."

The poor guy, Henry thought as he lay in bed. A few twisted fingers and he thinks he's a cripple. A simple piece of tail and he makes a production out of it. He thought of all the women he had had so effortlessly. Then an idea struck him as he remembered part of their conversation. He doesn't want to pay for it—well, what if he doesn't have to pay? In a few seconds, he had a plan.

"I'm probably the only twenty-one-year-old virgin in history," Jig was saying. "They ought to canonize me. Saint Jig."

Henry sensed the despair in the humor. "We'll work something out. Don't worry."

"Don't kill yourself," Jig muttered. "Goodnight."

The next afternoon, Henry withdrew fifty dollars from his bank account. It was a lot of money but what the hell, the poor bastard was desperate. He got to the Forty-Two Club at about ten o'clock that evening. It was a weeknight, and the place was not very crowded. A few of the girls had customers, a few were sitting alone at tables, one or two were at the bar. He chose a girl whose back view looked pretty good to him.

"Drinking alone?" She turned to him and smiled professionally.

Her intelligent good looks surprised him, they came through in spite of the thick make-up. She would do very well. Henry got right down to business. He asked her if she could use fifty dollars and had a few hours to spare. Yeah, she had lots of time and that's what she was there for. Then, he outlined his plan. She was to pretend that she was a friend of his and she was to allow Jig to seduce her.

"I don't want you to just lay back but, on the other hand, I don't want you to scare him off. He's got to think you like him. It's his first time and he's going to be scared."

"I got ya," she nodded. "He won't be the first I've had like that, all arranged I mean."

"Good," said Henry. "One more thing. This guy, my friend, Jig, has a bum hand. Don't draw any attention to it. It won't bother you, will it?"

She looked around her, her eyes taking in the whole bar. "You should see some of the poor creeps that come limping in here, hunchbacks, guys with stumps, and you should hear some of the things they ask us to do."

They left the bar and crossed the street over to the Paris Hotel. He paid the clerk seven dollars and they were shown a room. She stretched out on the bed as soon as the bellboy had left. Henry hadn't noticed that she looked that good.

"I think you better sit here," he said, indicating a chair in the corner. "Tell him that your baggage is arriving tomorrow, he's got to think you're a friend of mine. And do you think that you could get rid of some of that make-up? I think he prefers the homespun type."

While she was in the bathroom, Henry phoned his roommate.

"Jig, a friend of mine just got into town. I've been telling her about you, and she'd like to meet you. I think you'll like her. No, Jig, not another Patsy, just an ordinary friend. Paris Hotel, room 606. How soon can you make it? Good, then I'll expect you in a half-hour."

The girl emerged from the bathroom, almost beautiful without the make-up. There were droplets of water in her eyelashes.

"He'll be here in half an hour." He fished a roll of bills from his pocket. "Here's the fifty. You'll stay with him as long as he wants, won't you?"

She took the money and counted it. "Sure, I'll stay as long as he wants. You must think a lot of him to spend this kinda dough."

"He's a good guy and he has a rough time."

They sat down on the bed together. He noticed the firm, impressive bulge of her thighs, caught the scent of soap on her white flesh.

"Well, we've got about twenty minutes to kill."

"It's a rest for me," she said.

"You been in this business a long time?" he asked. "You look pretty young."

He was wondering about her body, its secrets and its textures.

"Long enough to make it hard to get out," she said indifferently. "Okay, okay," she said, when he moved against her, "only you'll have to make it fast if you don't want to surprise your buddy." She added a little wearily, "I suppose it's all on the same bill."

Ten minutes later, she was sitting dressed on the chair Henry had designated. Henry was leaning against the door, waiting, satisfied now that he had made a good choice for Jig. They heard the elevator.

"Say," he said, smiling at his classic question, "what's your name? I'll have to introduce you to him."

"Ramona. They call me Ray."

Jig knocked, and Henry opened the door.

"Jig, glad you could get here. I want you to meet my friend Ray. Ray, this is Jig."

"I've heard all about you," she said, smiling.

Henry lay in his bed. It was well past midnight and he hadn't heard from Jig yet. Well, finally he was getting his. Saint Jig. Henry chuckled, feeling a little saintly himself for having engineered the plan. He had been quite impressed with Ray and was certain that she could carry it through. Maybe he'd see her again himself in a week or two. After a while, he and Jig could laugh about it. Henry fell asleep, finally, congratulating himself.

The telephone rang at four-thirty that morning. Henry stumbled out of bed and stood by the desk. He knew who it was.

"Hi, Jig. You've certainly been at it a long time."

"Congratulate me, Hen." His voice was ecstatic.

"Congratulations, Jig," he said paternally. "Everything go all right?"

"Everything went beautifully. She's really a wonderful person, Ramona. Something just clicked between us."

Henry smiled. "Great. I'll see you soon and you can give me the details. Don't wear yourself out."

Jig went on as if he hadn't heard.

"And you know what, Hen? She doesn't care about my hand. Actually, she kissed it. Did you hear me? She kissed my hand."

Good for her, thought Henry. *She knows her trade*. "Okay, Jig, I'm glad it worked out. Tell me about it in the morning, I'm dead now."

"You can't go back to bed," Jig cried gleefully. "You've got to come down here."

"Thanks Jig, but I'm not interested right now. Save it for me."

"What do you mean, you're not interested? We're having a champagne breakfast. We want you here."

"I know this was important to you, Jig, but isn't this celebration a little out of proportion?" Henry laughed.

"Well, you don't get engaged every morning."

"What?"

"Engaged. I've asked her to marry me. I'm not going to let her walk out of my life."

Henry felt himself grow weak.

"Jig, I've got to talk to you. Just because a woman is good in bed, it doesn't mean that—"

Jig interrupted him sharply. "I wish you wouldn't talk about Ramona that way. After all, she's a friend of yours." Henry heard Jig cup the mouthpiece to muffle his voice. "I didn't go to bed with her, Henry. What do you think I am? There will be lots of time for that."

"Is she there?" Henry shouted angrily. "Put her on!"

"What's the matter with you? I thought you'd—"

"Put her on!"

Henry heard them exchange comments. She took the receiver.

"Listen, you little bitch, if you think—"

"Please," she whispered pathetically, "I'll return every cent—"

"Lemme talk to Jig. Jig, sta-stay right where you are. Don't move. I'll be right down!"

Henry sank into the chair beside the phone. He replaced the receiver, but he didn't get up for a long time.

O.K. Herb, O.K. Flo

All day, they carry their unwritten novels and unpainted pictures around in their heads. At night, they end up at the Shrine, on the corner of Sherbrooke and Victoria, and talk the ideas away. The jazz is poor but it's dark and maybe you'll be great tomorrow, and Christ! what crap the magazines are turning out. Later in the night, the city brings their failures back to them. The buildings, grey, solid, and religious, the buildings talk it into them with stone logic. Montreal is like a promise, an old Victorian promise that nobody dares to break. Or wants to break. The blackened lime-stone, the leering gargoyles, the iron gates seem to say, "You got a problem? Isn't that rough? Men suffer, buddy, and they suffer alone or else it isn't suffering. Go home alone. Walk on your own street and work it out." Of course, hardly anyone hears this. But I know a few spirits who hear it and they wander into the Shrine trying to forget it, or they stay home in their basements spilling their guts over poems or paint or eighty-eight keys until they learn to live with it. That's where I should have been. In my basement. Breaking my gonads over a sonnet. Cursing a hard sound into rhyme. Beating our clumsy language into a bird shape that could fly away. But I wasn't in my basement. I couldn't last an hour at my desk. The language was fighting back with phony

knuckles and dirty punches. "No bird shape for me," it screeched.
I got sick of the brawl. I hit Sherbrooke Street. Screw the language. Maybe it would tire itself while I was out and when I came
back later, it would be cuddling beside my typewriter and I'd stick
feathers in it and shove it out my window with a *Pax vobiscum.*
Sherbrooke Street. Elegant residential gone elegant commercial.
Churches strangled gracefully with tributaries of bare wines. Art
galleries for the churchgoers. All the stone you could want to
fool yourself that life is substantial. Steeples, spires, domes, pil-
lars. Everything touched by autumn, beautiful in the night and
very human. Wordsworth knew it when he finally got around to
looking at his own city: *Earth has not anything to show more fair. . . .*
And he knew about the slums too. The sound of wind and leaves
breaking their arched spines in the gutter. Now I was at the corner of Victoria. I could hear them blowing on the top floor of the
Shrine. Drums too loud. Trumpet too loud. I figured it was Herb.
Very flashy showman who waves his horn around like a sex symbol. Going over big with the Girls from Better Families who were
starting to trickle down to the Shrine for a thrill and some safe
dirt. Herb was pure grandstand and usually drunk. A noise in the
lane. Cross between a loud pop and a huge old hinge. Somebody
puking. A college kid grabbing at the side of the Shrine. Trying to
get his face against the stone for the coolness.

"Stay away from me," he wept, wiping a wet mouth with his
sleeve. "I don't have any money."

"Even if you did, it would be no bargain stinking of puke.
Here, take my arm. And keep your face turned the other way, will
you? You might not think much of this jacket, but it's seen me
through some very treacherous quatrains."

"What are you talking about? Quatrains. What are you doing?
Let go my arm."

"Just keep walking, Bacchus. To leeward of me."

Halfway round the block, we stopped for some retching action. It was probably his first drunk. He was a little proud. We exchanged names and occupations.

"You know what?" he said, with deep honesty, "I'm Secretary of the Debating Society."

"Want to buy a cheap speech?"

"No kidding, sir—" He started to call me sir. "No kidding, mister, I was just elected today. It's quite an honor for a freshman."

"For anybody."

"My father thought it was pretty good. He gave me fifteen dollars and told me to go downtown and celebrate."

"And you went downtown and celebrated. You're having a ball."

He was embarrassed and laughed. We were in front of the Shrine again.

"Going to make another assault or will you grab a taxi around the corner?"

He was fumbling in his pocket and trying to make a secret of it. He extended his hand to me like he wanted me to shake it. He had managed to fold a bill in his palm.

"I guess I better go home. I feel okay now, thanks to you. I want to thank you very much."

I shook his hand. He engineered the bill into mine. Then he was embarrassed again and beat it. Thank God, we still have our upper classes in Canada. They know how to treat their poor. Even though they need a little polish. I looked at the bill. It was a ten.

"Wait a second, Mr. Secretary," I shouted.

He froze on the corner till I got to him. I'm sure he didn't know whether I'd smash him or embrace him.

"I think you over changed me. Look."

"Oh, I meant—" He pulled a bill out of his pocket in a panic. "I, I thought the two was on top—"

At that moment his suffering was monumental. Then he recovered himself. Breeding came through. *Noblesse oblige.* He took a deep breath and gurgled a bit to find a voice.

"That's quite all right. I want you to have it."

"Now listen, friend, just because you made a mistake—"

He started to panic again. "No, no, it's yours. I tell you, it's yours. I've got to get home now." Another minor recovery: "And if ever I can help you out again—"

But he couldn't finish. He pushed my hand with the ten in it, and away he fled.

"Thanks," I called after him, "and save me a place on your Cabinet."

Poor kid. Pride, you murdering bastard. Up in the Shrine, Herb was grinding out the ending he uses for every bit. Applause. Mostly female, I figured, as I climbed the stairs. Place was dark as usual. Deep red lights gave everyone an unhealthy tan. Few couples taking advantage and making out. The musicians were quitting for their break. Being very casual with the ringsiders. Like they were just regular fellows and the audience was every bit as good as they were. But with smirks that betrayed. I flipped the kid's bill on the table.

"Why don't you birds spend a buck and turn on some real lights. That's a ten."

"Hey sport," said the moneychanger, "what happened to you? Finally made the Nobel Prize?"

"Very clever, Mister Hurok. Eight, nine, ten. Thank you."

"Herb wants to see you. He's up front, with a chick."

"Who's Herb?"

And I headed for a table in the far corner. But I met him ten minutes later in the men's room. There's no escaping Herb. What he wanted was for me to write some publicity copy for his group.

"You know I don't do that kind of stuff."

"Sorry, poet man, I thought that jazz was one of the few things you approved of."

He was drunk and buzzing with something more than alcohol.

"That's right, Herb. Jazz, I approve of. Not the sexy hoax, you guys are blowing with your lower torsos and eyebrows."

"You're the one to talk, poet man, with your slim obscure volumes, thick as a forest, with breasts and thighs. Yessir, Mister Moral, preach me a little bit."

"I would if I thought you ever listened to anything anybody ever said. The difference between my stuff and yours is that my breasts and thighs run through with blood and muscle and are attached to warm human frames, which think and love and hate. Yours are disembodied aphrodisiacs, aimed at tickling the naughty bones of bored chicks who are too lazy even to use a candle."

I caught my face in the mirror. Portrait of the Poet Wasting His Time. What the hell was I doing in a green lavatory arguing a stupid point with someone I didn't like and who wasn't listening? That's what I can't stand about Herb. Somehow, he always gets me to talk Art. Herb leaned on the wall and closed his eyes. I knew I was in for a barrage.

"Before you start, Herb—"

"The trouble with you, poet man, is that too many years of being left unread, too many years of literary neglect, too many years of scratching in quicksand—"

"O.K. Herb, cut the rhetoric, spit it out."

"Too many years of scratching in quicksand, etching in water, scribbling on wind—"

"For Christ's sake!"

"Scribbling on wind, chalking on whitewash, carving in waterfalls—"

There's no stopping Herb when he gets like this. He doesn't hear you anyway. His own words work with the booze and goof-balls and he's moving on a very far out level. I flicked some water in his face. He came out of it.

"What's the use," he said.

"I agree, Herb. What's the use?"

For the first time, I saw something that looked like pain on Herb's face. Usually, he has a vicious, drugged, handsome air about him. I figured he must have been talking about himself. There's no neglect like the neglect awarded to a local performer. No matter how loud the chicks squeal. He flung his arm over my shoulder. Something I can't stand from anybody.

"Listen, poet man, this is a big night for me."

"Don't tell me. Let me guess. You were elected President of the Debating Society."

Of course, he didn't hear me.

"I got Mac's wife with me."

"She used to go with you before she married Mac, didn't she?"

"Mac is crippled now."

"Yeah, I heard. Streetcar, wasn't it?"

"There are only two things a girl can give you," Herb went on. "The first is her virginity. That, I got from her a long time ago. The second is her fidelity, her husband's trust. That, I get from her tonight. Her very first episode in adultery."

"Take your arm off me, will you, Herb? You know I can't stand it."

"She's going to have to get it somewhere, with Mac like he is. It might as well be me. There are a hundred guys hanging around already."

"Who're you trying to convince, Herb?"

"If you promise not to do any preaching, I'll invite you over to our table. Oh, c'mon poet man, Montreal's Frail Child, your stomach can take it."

"No thanks, Herb."

"Please," he said in a voice a little too desperate for the situation.

We got to the table. He half-led me, half-leaned on me. She looked uncomfortable. As if she didn't want to meet anyone she knew.

"Hi, Flo," I said, "how's Mac?"

Herb glared at me.

"You trying to be funny?" said Flo.

"Let's everybody sit down," said Herb. "The next set will be on in a minute."

"Make it another Pernod for me, Herb."

"That'll make it five. Are you sure, Flo?"

Flo turned to me, "Isn't he the soul of concern. I guess he's afraid I won't be able to perform. Don't worry, Herb, you got it made."

Flo got her drink. I had some Bristol Cream. To remind me of better days. Herb paid and then left us to go to the stand. Before he left, he dug a fist between her thighs. She caught her breath and flushed. The music began. Piano first. Dull. He was playing for himself. Didn't give a damn. Neither did the drums. Hi-hat clicking automatically. Herb pretended to listen to the other men. Bell of the horn flat on his stomach and grinding his hips.

"I suppose he told you," said Flo. "Can't keep his bloody mouth shut. Never could."

"Here's to Herb."

Herb was blowing aloud and uneasy, as if he were signalling the piano to help him out.

"Christ, I hate him," said Flo. "I could only do this with someone I hate. Seems fairer to Mac."

"How is Mac, anyway?"

She made her lips thin and white.

"You know bloody well how Mac is. What are you trying to prove? Mac's a cripple from his bellybutton down. That's how Mac is."

Then I heard the bass. He was great. Travelling up and down the scale with big easy leaps. Like he was trying to herd the group together.

"Listen to that bass," I told her.

Under his high tilted horn, Herb swayed dizzily. The musicians didn't get any better. The bass tried like crazy to the very end. Herb came back to the table. Before he sat down, he gobbled a goofball and washed it down with what was left of Flo's Pernod. He pinched her rump and sat down.

"I'd go easy on those," said Flo.

"You're right," said Herb thickly. "Encourages the appetite, deadens the instrument."

He lowered his face to the table and licked her arm with his tongue, from the inside elbow to the wrist. His chin slid off her hand onto the table. She was breathing heavily. In heat. He was asleep. I shook him, but it was no use. We watched him for a minute or two. His nostrils breathing halfmoons of mist on the shiny table. With a clenched fist, Flo was kneading her belly.

"And he was worried about me," she said bitterly. "I guess it serves me right. I guess—" But she didn't finish. There were tears running down her cheeks and her shoulders were trembling. "What the hell am I doing here, whoring around the Shrine with a drunk trumpet, what am I doing here?" She leaned into my arms in despair and I took pleasure in her woman's weight. "I've got to get home," she pleaded. "Mac must be worrying about me." She hung on to my arm. Frail and forlorn. Wiping her nose as we made our way out.

"Better take a look at Herb," I told the moneychanger.

"Don't worry about Herb, sport. Never missed a set in his life."

"Well, this time he's out for good."

We went down the stairs very slowly. I helped her with each one. I was tender because of her misery. At every descent, our bodies became closer. Beside the door, we embraced. For a long time. People went by us. I noticed them, but she didn't. And I wasn't thinking of her misery anymore. I was thinking that she was going to have to get it somewhere, that there were a hundred guys hanging around already.

"You don't know what it's like," she wept. "And he tries so hard, Mac tries so hard."

"I know, I know," I told her automatically.

I was thinking what a mess my room was and how long ago it was that I changed my sheets. We went outside. Our nostrils opened to the cold. You couldn't see the buildings right away. The streetlamps were too bright. She had my arm in both her hands. Her face against my sleeve. Then we heard the horn. Herb's horn. Coming through the night like a silver stab. I never heard him blow like that before. He was saying, yes, yes, yes. It was strong and humble and confident. I thought, "He must've played like that a long time ago." He called the piano and it came like a steady rickshaw under his sound. He summoned the drums and they were a buzz saw cutting the brush, so Herb could travel, striking stumps of cut crystal on the way. And the bass moved around everything like a throbbing guarding sky. "That's what making a decision will do for you," I said to myself. She didn't change the position of her hands on my arm, but I felt something change. In the fingers. It was desire leaking away.

"The bastard must have been faking," she said, astonished. "Wonder why he wanted to do a thing like that."

"Maybe to give you a chance of getting out of the situation."

She dropped her hands to her sides. The two of us stood for a long while listening to the music and the fragile scrape of the leaves in their last season.

"It's funny," she said. "Now that I come to think of it, Herb pulled something like this the very first night we spent together. We were getting undressed when he remembered he'd left the keys in the car. I heard the motor start and he didn't come back for five hours. Now I see why. To give me a chance to get out."

"Do you want to go back in?" I asked, as softly as possible.

She answered too quickly and there was a trace of panic in her voice. "No, no, we're together now. I left the place with you. I'm with you now." But what she really said, what she said with her hurt eyes and her trembling was, "Oh, God, I'm sick of this mess. Please let's go over to your place and get this thing over with. I've wounded you up like a cheap whore, and you deserve to have me. I'm an adulteress and I haven't the right to choose my men. At least let me do one decent thing."

And I suppose I would have taken her, desire or not, because at that moment she was very beautiful in her panic, in her autumn, a child of the darkness and the music around us. But she made me remember a puking kid and a ten-dollar bill. I took both her hands and I said, "Look, Flo, don't be afraid of asking for something back. Especially something you let go by mistake."

She was about to protest. To let her pride flourish. But she stopped and thought about what I had said. She understood what I meant.

"You're not committed to me," I said, to reinforce the meaning. "It takes more than a few kisses and heavy breathing."

I hoped she'd laugh, and she did. She kissed my cheek and I walked her back to the door of the Shrine. Herb was still blowing strong and fine.

"Isn't he great?"

"I suppose he is," I said.

"I like him very much."

"I hope you do."

"I feel like I've never been with a man before."

"Good."

"Sorry to have got you into this for nothing, I mean, to have let you—"

"Don't worry about it, Flo. Good luck."

Back to Sherbrooke Street. The blackened limestone, the leering gargoyles, the iron gates were saying what they always said. To me. To no one else. The leaves were swirling into crisp nests in the gutter. O.K. Herb, O.K. Flo, go to it. O.K. Mac, work it out, somehow. I have my own instructions. The churches and stores were dark and old but stood with dignity. I stopped and took in the scene around me. Looking for a poem to put me to sleep.

Signals

"Drive along Westmount Boulevard, will you, Fred, since we have nowhere special to go."

"What's along Westmount Boulevard?"

"A house. A window I used to watch."

"Whose window? A maiden in a tower? An imprisoned love?"

"That sort of thing. House of the family Greenbell. I told you about Judith."

"Haven't we celebrated that tragedy already, Lyon? I recall at least ten toasts drunk to her damnation when you heard she had been married in England last week."

"That was last week. She's in town now."

"With husband?"

"With husband. Her parents are giving them a reception to which I wasn't invited. Neither was Herson."

"Do you expect a woman to invite her former lover and his friends to her wedding reception?"

"Yes. I would expect her to invite the closest friends she had in this city. She hasn't got in touch with us, and I can't seem to get her on the phone. There was never any bitterness between us. We just drifted apart, that's all. Too bad you never knew her."

"She left before I came."

"You would have been in love with her, like the rest of us."

"You were in love with her?"

"Well, as close as I come to love."

"Which isn't very close, considering the women you've gone through in the past year."

"Close enough for her."

"Apparently not."

"She would have married me if I wanted. I was the one who stopped answering letters."

"Why?"

"What was the use of stretching the affair on and on? She was a woman ready for marriage, needing marriage . . ."

"And you were just a youth, a follower after beauty, the golden boy of a brief episode."

"That sort of thing. There's the house. The lighted window is her room. Drive slowly. Slower. Did you see anyone in her room?"

"I was watching the road."

"I haven't seen a light in that room for a year."

"Do you often look?"

"Yes, I often look."

The two young men drove in silence. Fred found music on the radio. They drove along streets that gave views of the lights of the city and its bridges below. Lyon looked in the windows of the great houses they passed, catching glimpses of family TV here, a solitary reader there.

"I love driving at night," said Lyon. "You are part of everything and part of nothing at the same time. Driving up and down these streets, we're like a thick black needle stitching the city into our brains but with no suffering involved. Everything belongs to us, but we own nothing."

"Do you want to stop at the lookout?"

"No, let's keep on going. When you stop, you're just some-thing another passing car can include in its journey."

"Let's not get mystical."

"Judith loved this route."

"I suppose you told her all about the black needles and being part of everything and nothing?"

"No. She told me."

"I know the type."

"What type?"

"The type that sees mystery in everything, the type that is always having mystical relationships with everything, whose vocab-ulary is full of words like *being* and *becoming* and *communion*."

"Don't forget *love*."

"Oh, yes, *love*. *Love* everything. And *suffering*. That's another one of their words. *Infinitely suffering*. Also *wounded*."

"It's amazing how wrong you are. She wasn't wounded, and she wasn't suffering. She laughed, and you laughed, and anyone who was around laughed. She wore what she wanted, and she said what she wanted, and still, she was always a woman."

"Now I really do know the type. She could say *shit* without blushing and probably said it often. She wore white running shoes, black knee socks, and had a ponytail. She liked Bartok and folk songs, the Chinese poems of Ezra Pound, and wept with Carson McCullers when she wasn't taking Modern Dance lessons."

"You know, Fred, you've been living in the Left Banks and Greenwich Villages of too many cities. She didn't take lessons in Modern Dance and she didn't look like an American college exis-tentialist. Sometimes, her hair was arranged so intricately that I just sat and stared at it as though it was some beautiful forbid-den puzzle. Sometimes, when I picked her up at her house and she came down the stairs dressed in something out of Humbert

Wolfe, I would wonder who she was and if it could possibly be me that she was expecting."

"Who the hell is Humbert Wolfe?"

"No one very clever. An English civil servant who died a few years ago. Nobody in your espressos ever heard of him."

"That sounds properly esoteric."

"Alright, make whatever picture you want of her. I'll just remember her coming down the stairs or climbing out of Lac Masson and brushing her hair dry in the sun."

"*The Birth of Venus.*"

"That sort of thing. Let's drop in on Herson."

"That hard-drinking man? I thought you wanted to go for a drive."

"Herson knew her and I want to talk to someone who knew her."

"We're really going to indulge ourselves, aren't we?"

"Ah! Gentlemen, come right in. You've interrupted the greatest short story of the year, but what is that beside the company of friends. Sit down in my clever round modern chairs and assist me in an experiment."

He placed on the low glass table a bottle of vodka, a bottle of vermouth, a tray of ice and glasses.

"I am about to make a vodka martini."

"What is so experimental about a vodka martini?" asked Lyon.

"Patience, patience, my young singer. Here you are Fred, and here you are Lyon. Well, gentlemen, shall we propose a toast?"

"I'm sure Lyon has a suggestion. This has been Nostalgia Night all over America."

"I see," said Herson. "Well, then gentlemen: may I give you the lovely Judy Greenbell?"

They clinked their glasses.

"Judith Greenbell. She hated Judy."

"A thousand pardons, Lyon. Unfortunately, I was never intimate with the young lady's preferences. Well, then gentlemen: the lovely Judith Greenbell."

Again, they clinked their glasses.

"Well, gentlemen, what do you think of it?" He leaned back with a look of triumph.

"It tastes very much like a vodka martini."

"Just as I thought. And you, Lyon?"

"I agree with Fred. It tastes very much like a vodka martini."

"Aha!"

"Well, what's the great experiment?"

"Classified, gentlemen, highly classified. The Russians must never find out. Here, let me fill your glasses. To Lyon and Judith who were the most beautiful summer lovers I shall ever know. To their eternal memory."

"We're going to get sloshed very quickly drinking like this," said Lyon.

"An excellent idea," said Herson. He refilled their glasses. "An excellent idea."

Lyon settled in his chair and drank thoughtfully.

"Why do you think she didn't invite us to the reception? If there was anybody in the city, I thought it would be us she'd invite."

"Perhaps we were her bohemian chapter. Every woman has in her life a bohemian chapter which she wants to forget. Or to remember."

"Oh, very bohemian," said Lyon sarcastically, taking in with a sweep of his hand the expensive apartment and his well-dressed companions.

Herson answered him quickly and in his voice, there was a touch of anger, which surprised Lyon.

"Look, Lyon, I'd have thought you would be tired of talking about her by this time. You've been here every night this week, with her name painfully hanging on your lips, and full of regret. After all, the thing only lasted a month. Lovely as it might have been, a brief summer love can't be mourned a lifetime, not if you want to keep your friends."

"Bravo," said Fred.

Herson filled their glasses again. They drank in silence. Herson brooded regretfully over what he had said.

"But I understand," he said finally. "Sad old Herson under-stands everything because sad old Herson too once loved a summertime away when he was your age, young and easy, and full of life."

"Very touching," said Fred.

"Why weren't we invited, Herson? Think of the time she spent with us, the things she told us."

"The things she told you," corrected Herson.

"Was she really all that beautiful?" asked Fred.

Herson nodded his head slowly. "She was really all that beau-tiful. They were both beautiful. They walked along Ste. Catherine Street holding hands. They wrote each other bad poetry. They had secrets and signals. Did he tell you how he would pick her up at night? He would bring her home around midnight. That was for her parents' sake. Then, he would pass by a couple of hours later. If there was a light in her window, and three or four times a week there was, that meant everything was clear. He would stop the car and open and close the door twice. That was the signal. Tell Fred about it, Lyon, tell the philistine about love."

Lyon continued enthusiastically. "At my signal, she would come to the window. She would not be wearing anything, and she would stand in the dim window, and both of us would watch each other, and I have never seen anything so beautiful. Then she would disappear into the room and dress. The light would go out and a moment later she was down the stairs and into the car, smelling of her bath."

"Sounds like Lorca," said Fred. "An urban adaptation."

"Have some more of my experiment," said Herson. "And tell us about her letters. You're going to, anyway."

"Her letters were beautiful. They were written on thin blue paper with green ink and were always sad. The second to last one said: '*I would send you a piece of the sky, but you would not know whom it was from.*' Isn't that beautiful?"

"Aren't you tired of that word?" asked Herson, with sudden contempt.

"What word?"

"*Beautiful. Beautiful. Beautiful. Beautiful.* That word."

"Take it easy, Herson," said Fred.

"You're drunk," said Lyon.

"Where did you go after she got into your car?" asked Fred quickly.

Herson answered, facing Lyon as he spoke.

"Here. The lovers came here. I would chat with them for a few minutes and then I'd mercifully leave them for an hour or two, for a long drink at the Tour."

"What's the matter with you, Herson? I've never heard you talking like this. I never thought you minded us coming here. I thought you sort of liked it."

"I loved it, Lyon. I loved it. After all, it was your turn."

"What are you talking about?"

Herson stood up and walked to the window. Fred and Lyon watched him stand there, leaning wearily against the wall, his hands in his pockets. He had never looked so old to Lyon. *Why, he must be forty-five*, he thought suddenly.

"Gentlemen," Herson began, "I can no longer withhold from you the contents of your vodka martini."

"Never mind the martini," said Lyon. "What did you mean just then?"

"It is not vodka at all, gentlemen. It is pure alcohol obtained for me by a chemist friend. Up to now, no one has been able to tell the difference."

"Congratulations, Doctor Pasteur."

"Thank you, Fred," he said bowing. "I see Lyon is unimpressed. Perhaps the achievement does not coincide with his idea of the world of natural beauty."

"You're not making sense, Herson," said Lyon.

"Of course, my world is sordid. I'm middle-aged and a hack writer, so naturally my world is sordid. I don't have signals that bring naked girls to windows. I'm not twenty with a manuscript of love lyrics. I'm forty with a load of alcohol and a black book of conquests."

"What's the matter, Herson? Tell me," said Lyon, going over to him.

"But into every sordid life, a little sex must fall. And I even got letters. She sent me a letter last week. Green ink on thin blue paper, just like you said. And very sad."

"Judith sent you a letter? What did she say?"

"She said I would have to tell you, or she couldn't face either of us."

"Tell me what, for God's sake?" There was fear in his voice.

"Tell you that, on alternate nights, she came down here without the benefit of you or car doors or lighted windows."

"You're lying."

"That's right, Lyon. I'm lying. Don't believe a word I've said. God's in his heaven and all's right with the world."

"You mean, she slept with you?"

"Generally. Sometimes, I was too drunk. That was my role: dissolute drunkard. Your role was golden boy poet. She had a wide range of taste."

"I don't believe you. You're drunk, and this is another of your playing-with-people games."

"You're perfectly right. Don't believe me. If I were you, I wouldn't believe me. But I had to tell you anyway. And don't look so threateningly at me. You'll scare an old man."

Lyon turned and ran into the bathroom. They heard him throw up.

"Take him home," Herson said to Fred. "You have just witnessed a youth emerging from adolescence and an adolescent emerging into middle age. I've wanted to do it all week. My ersatz vodka finally did the trick."

"An interesting girl," said Fred. "I'd love to meet her."

"To meet her is to love her."

Lyon came back into the room, his face white.

"I hate you, Herson," he said quietly.

"Soon you won't. Good night, gentlemen."

There was a fine rain falling. The two young men drove in silence.

"Take Westmount Boulevard home, will you, Fred."

"Aren't you tired of fairy tales after tonight?"

"I want to see the house once more. Tonight will be the last time. I can promise you that."

"You mean this morning. It's two o'clock."

"And go slowly this time."

"Don't worry, Prince Charming. I'm far too drunk to speed."

"I can't get it out of my mind, her lying in bed with Herson all that month."

"Try her lying in bed right now with her husband."

"I can't get that out of my mind either."

The car rolled slowly between the great stone houses of Westmount. The streetlamps dripped into their own puddles of light. Lyon rolled down the window and laid his cheek on the cool wet steel of the door. He remembered the frozen waves of her intricate hair and the drops of water on her shoulders, and more intimate things such as the curve of her thigh and the mound of her stomach, but these thoughts finally led to visions of enemy lovers and he was almost sick again. The houses were familiar now, the ones he had counted so many times. Four more would be her house.

"Oh, my God, Fred, stop. The light, the light's in the window!"

Fred stopped the car and leaned over to look out of Lyon's window.

"So it is. This is insane. What are you going to do?"

"I don't know."

They both watched the dimly lit window, Fred's chin on Lyon's shoulder. A few minutes passed.

"Yes, I do know. Move over."

Fred resumed his driver's position. Lyon opened and closed the car door twice. They waited.

"It's her. Oh, God, it's her. She's in the window."

Fred leaned over and caught a glimpse of a vague form before Lyon pushed him back.

"Don't look, Fred. Please, don't look."

Lyon opened the door and got out.

"Is she wearing anything?"

"No. Now she's waving."

"Just remember, her husband's in that room."

"I can't see her now. She's gone back into the room."

"This is insane. Is she going to come down?"

"The light's gone."

He climbed back into the car.

"Let's get out of here."

"Look, Lyon, if you want to hang around, you can have the car and I'll grab a taxi. There's no point in—"

But he stopped when he saw the tears glisten on Lyon's cheek.

"Get going, Fred, get going."

He laid his head on the window as before. As the car sped away, the warm tears instantly turned cool on his cheek.

"The whore," he repeated over and over, "the dirty whore."

Polly

I waited until I was certain Polly would be home from school and then I ran up my street toward her house. When I reached her driveway, I could already hear her wooden flute. I could have stayed there and listened to all the music I wanted, but I walked on into her backyard. She was seated deep in a large garden chair, her head back, her eyes closed, and the instrument held high and lightly against her lips. I listened for another moment until she heard me. She opened her eyes and stopped playing, but she didn't remove the wooden flute from her lips.

"You here again? What for this time?" she buzzed.

"Same as before. To hear your wooden flute."

"It's not a wooden flute," she said, with great contempt, "it's a recorder. Can't you remember that? Recorder. I've never even heard of a wooden flute."

"I could have stayed in the driveway without you ever knowing and listened to you play," I told her, hoping to impress her with my honesty.

"Well then, why didn't you?"

"I don't know. I thought it wouldn't be fair."

"Well, you know what you have to do if you want to come around here."

Polly always spoke to me that way, as if she didn't like me and I bothered her. But I knew that I was practically her only friend. When we went to grade school, we always walked home together. She was three grades ahead of me, and now she attended the junior high and she always walked home alone. She dropped the instrument into her lap and tapped it with her fingers as she spoke.

"Let's see. What'll I make you do today for your song? What did I make you do yesterday?"

"I had to find out how many somersaults could be done from one end of the lawn to the other."

"Yes, I remember. And how many were there?"

"About eighteen. I forget exactly."

"You forget! Do you think I set these tasks for nothing? You just better find out again how many there were."

"Now? Right away?"

"Right away, if you ever want to hear another note of music."

I walked to the garage wall. She didn't turn around to watch me. I kneeled down and somersaulted past her to the edge of the lawn, and then returned to where she was sitting.

"Eighteen."

"That's what you said in the first place," she reminded me.

"Will you play now?" I asked, brushing my clothes with my hands.

"That was yesterday's. You've still got to do today's. And I haven't decided what today's will be yet."

"Please decide, Polly," I said solemnly, wondering if the music was worth the humiliation after all.

"All right," she said, "I want a bouquet of dandelions. Eighteen dandelions so you won't forget the somersaults. And the bunch has to be tied up with red string. A bouquet of dandelions, that's what you have to get for today."

And she folded her arms on her chest. I remembered seeing a cluster of dandelions when I had kneeled beside the garage. I picked seven there. Across the fence, I saw some yellow flowers among the bushes, but I discovered that they were chrysanthemums.

"Not chrysanthemums," Polly called at me, "dandelions. Can't you remember?"

The sky was getting dark. I knew that soon I could be called for dinner.

"Seven wouldn't do, just for today?" I asked feebly.

Polly didn't even answer. I took a shortcut across a few fences to the field beside the Layton's. Sheila, a girl in my class, was playing there by herself.

"Sheila," I cried, "help me gather some dandelions."

"What for?" she asked, following me from flower to flower.

"I've got to get a bouquet for something. Hurry, please."

Sheila was unsatisfied with my answer, but she ran off and returned with a handful of the precious blossoms.

"Here," she said, "now tell me, what for?"

"Tomorrow," I said, snatching them from her and running off.

"O.K. for you," she called after me.

I was halfway back to Polly's when I remembered the red string. I raced to my own house where I knew there was some on the kitchen table.

"Oh, are those for me? How nice," my mother said.

"No, no," I spluttered, "but I'll get you a bouquet soon, I will."

"That's all right. What do you want? A glass to put them in?"

"Just a piece of red string to tie them up with," I said, getting what I wanted from the kitchen drawer.

Polly smiled when I approached.

"Eighteen," she said, after counting them.

"Very good. All right, what do you want to hear?"

"'Alas, my love'. . . . Same as yesterday."

"You mean 'Greensleeves' Lady Greensleeves. Can't you remember anything?"

Polly adjusted her position so that she couldn't see me. I lay on my back, looking up at the darkening sky. Then the music began. Sky, leaves, garage, grass, everything seemed to lean on us as if the music were a thin powerful wire, pulling everything together. I closed my eyes. Polly played the song through a few times and then started to play her own song. She entered into her own tune, so softly that I hardly realized she was no longer playing 'Greensleeves.' Yes, the somersaults and flowers meant nothing, and Polly was right in asking for them. No, I just couldn't sit by her anytime and have her play for me. Some gift had to be made. Raindrops fell on my face, but I waited until I could feel them through my shirt before opening my eyes. Polly stopped playing and looked at me as if I were responsible for the rain.

"We could go into the garage," I suggested quietly.

Polly got up and opened the small garage door and disappeared inside without motioning me to follow. I heard the music start again. Lady Greensleeves. I entered and closed the small door behind me. It was very dark and smelt of oil and last year's leaves, some of which I crushed underfoot. I could barely make out Polly, who was sitting on some old crates and leaning against the damp wall. I sat down a few feet from her. The music was much louder in the garage. It filled up the stone room like a flood. I could hear nothing but the song and the rain against the small high windows of the sliding door. After a very few minutes, she stopped playing and announced that I'd better go home now because she was putting the recorder away and because she'd had enough of me anyway. I opened the door for her and we both went out into the yard. It was raining very lightly. She put the instrument under her blouse to protect it.

"Will the rain hurt it?" I asked, trying to show interest and gratitude.

"'Will the rain hurt it, will the rain hurt it?'" she mocked. "What do you think the rain will do? Help it? Turn it into gold?"

"I guess not," I said, and she began to mount the stairs into her house.

"Thank you, Polly," I called after her. "Can I come tomorrow?"

"Aren't you ever going to leave me alone?"

The next day she wouldn't see me at all. As soon as I came into the yard, she went into her house. I went over to the field beside Layton's. Sheila was there, playing with her skipping rope.

"More dandelions?" she sang out.

"Nope," I said, as she came over to me.

"You promised me you'd tell me what they were for."

"I didn't promise, but I'll tell you anyhow," I said, happy to recount the experience. "It was so Polly would play the wooden flute to me." And I told her about the dandelions and the rain and the garage.

"Well, if that's the way she treats people, it's no wonder she doesn't have any friends." Still, Sheila was interested, and she asked if maybe she couldn't come along one afternoon.

"We can try tomorrow," I said, immediately sorry for my words because I knew it wasn't a thing that should be shared. Besides, I thought that Polly would be angry.

The following afternoon, we presented ourselves to Polly. As we were turning into the driveway, we could hear the music and Sheila wanted to stay right there and listen to it without any trouble, but I would hear nothing of this. Polly was seated as usual in her wooden chair. She stopped playing as I approached.

"I brought a friend. This is Sheila," I said to Polly.

"Hello, Polly," Sheila said.

"I hope you didn't bring her here for me to entertain the both of you. I'm not an organ-grinder. You alone are bad enough," she said to me, ignoring Sheila altogether.

But I could see that Polly was actually flattered that I had brought her another spectator. I wondered what she would make the both of us do.

"Do you like music, Sheila?" Polly asked, lightly prodding her in the stomach with the instrument.

"Well, yes, I like it, I guess."

"You guess. Did he tell you what he had to do?"

"You mean about the somersaults and the dandelions? Yes, he told me. I helped him pick some of them."

"You helped him pick some?"

She leaned towards me. "You little cheat. You didn't tell me anybody helped you." I said that I didn't think it mattered. "Of course, it matters, you're just a cheat. Well, you're not going to get away with anything this time if you want to hear me play."

"What do you want us to do?" I said, looking at Sheila, who, I thought, must be sorry she had come in the first place.

"Let me see," Polly said, sinking back into her chair and looking at the two of us.

"Here, Sheila, let me see that skipping rope."

Sheila handed it to her. Polly got up and tied one end around my waist and the other end around Sheila's waist so that we were bound about a foot from one another. We were both too curious to protest.

"Now just wait a second," Polly said, and ran up the stairs into her house. She returned with some newspaper which she began to roll up. "Have you a handkerchief?" she asked me.

I gave her my handkerchief and she blindfolded Sheila.

"Hey, what is this?" Sheila cried.

I assured her that nothing bad would happen and she submitted. The fact is we were both fascinated by the whole ritual.

"Now the idea is," Polly said, placing a roll of newspaper in each of Sheila's hands, "the idea is that when I start blowing, you start bashing him with the newspaper and you don't stop until I stop blowing." And she said to me, "You must keep your hands in your pockets."

I watched Polly. She looked at me as she removed the mouthpiece from the instrument and put it to her lips. She blew hard and it sounded high and harsh. Sheila brought one roll lightly down on my shoulder. Polly stepped very close to Sheila and blew the mouthpiece right beside her ear. She began to squeal and rain blows down on my head and shoulders. Polly never took her eyes off me during the whole thing. Then the whistle stopped, but Sheila didn't, and I had to catch hold of both her hands. I seemed to be the only one at all upset. Sheila was grinning, and Polly seemed satisfied.

"Will you play for us now, Polly?" I asked.

"The garage. In the garage," Sheila whispered to me. Polly heard.

"So, you told her about that too? You don't know anything about secrets, do you?" Polly strode to the garage door and pushed it open. "All right, you two. Get in, if you want to."

We followed her, and I closed the door behind us. There was the same damp autumn smell and it brought back to me the afternoon two days past. I could hardly wait for the music to begin. I wondered if it would be the same with Sheila there. Polly took her old seat and Sheila and I settled ourselves a little distance away. The music began and soon it filled the whole garage, overwhelming me. It called into our stone room the vast night from the other side of the world. I reached for Sheila's hand. As soon as my fingers touched hers, she took my hand between both her hands and pressed it against her mouth. Then she leaned against my shoulder and kissed my cheek. I wanted to join my voice with the flute's. I held her close against me. I knew no afternoon we would ever spend would be as beautiful as this. In the week that followed, we visited Polly almost every day. And every day, we submitted ourselves to the humiliations Polly had prepared. Soon, I hardly knew whether I came for the music or the secret embrace which the music and the darkness allowed. There was no such division on Sheila's mind.

"Why do we want to put up with all her nonsense for?" she said. "We could meet without her, in your garage or mine?"

But I wasn't at all ready to give up the music and Sheila knew it was no use arguing with me. So, we continued to visit Polly, always careful to show her the greatest respect. She suspected nothing. She thrived on us. She never spoke except to give us a command or call us down. Although she knew nothing of our movements in the dark, she seemed to sense how much we needed her, or at any rate, how much I needed her. Arrogant as she became, I was ready to do whatever she willed. One afternoon, our task involved finding a broken yoyo which Polly had hidden at the bottom of one of the garbage cans underneath her back steps. Sheila refused to assist me as I removed each soaked, smelling package. Polly didn't seem to mind. I had to turn away

from the search several times to prevent myself from retching.
I finally found the toy.

"It's about time," Polly said.

Sheila was disgusted with me and I felt terribly degraded
myself. I didn't know what to say.

"You'd better wash your hands before we begin," Polly ordered
me.

When I returned, we took our places in the garage. Polly
began her music and when I felt that she was caught up with it
and knew that her eyes were closed and her heart part of the
sound, I drew Sheila towards me. And with the damp bricks
ringing, the oil glistening in dark rainbows and the leaves softly
splintering under my tapping shoe, we loved with all our eleven-
year-old passion. Sheila was not so affected by the atmosphere.
I was her real interest, and this afternoon, she was bolder than
she had ever been. She began to tickle me in the ribs.

"Careful, careful," I barely whispered in her ear.

"'Careful, careful,'" she mocked, brushing my cheek with her
lips. Then she kissed me loudly on my nose.

"Sheila, Sheila, she'll hear us," I whispered desperately.

And then suddenly, we were both of us laughing out loud,
unable to contain ourselves, exhilarated by our impudence. The
music stopped abruptly. Polly ran across the garage and switched
on an electric light I had never noticed. Sheila and I were still
in each other's arms. In a second, Polly understood the deception
we had practised on her the past week, how we had used her to
excuse our embraces and why we had so cunningly endured her
insults. And in her deep humiliation and pain, with both hands
she pressed the flute across her eyes and sank to a sitting position
in the oil and dirt of the floor of the garage, her body trembling.

"You two. You two," was all she could manage.

"Oh, Polly," I began, kneeling beside her, not knowing what to say. "Start again, please start again. This time we'll really listen, won't we, Sheila?"

Sheila walked to the door of the garage and opened it. With one hand, Polly pushed me away using as much strength as she could muster. I followed Sheila out of the garage.

"You two!" Polly screamed after us.

"No wonder she has no friends," Sheila said, as she walked down the street. "No wonder she has to walk home alone."

But I was not prepared to discuss the awful thing that had just happened and after I had made an appointment to meet her the next day after school, I walked home for dinner. Sheila and I met in my garage, as we had planned the day before. She had arrived before me and had arranged dome boxes for us to sit on. I sat down, and she put her head against my shoulder and squeezed my hand.

"Now we're all by ourselves," she whispered.

It seemed so pointless, the two of us sitting there in that half-lit garage, our slightest movements and whispers echoing the silence back to us that I could hardly sit still.

"What's the matter?" she asked. "Don't you like me still?"

"Course I like you. It's just that I can't stay, that's all. I have to do something for my mother. We're having company and I have to go downtown and pick up some flowers for the tables," I lied.

"Well, why didn't you tell me yesterday?"

"I didn't remember yesterday."

And I fled from the garage, leaving Sheila pouting in the darkness. As I walked up the street, I wondered what I would say to Polly, and what she would say to me. I lingered for a few minutes in the driveway, listening to the music, then I walked to the backyard. She was sitting as usual in the wooden chair. She looked up at me and continued playing. I sat down on the grass, not far from her. When she had finished her song, she said, "You know, I had to remove all the garbage and then put it back to hide the yoyo in the first place."

"Oh, Polly," I said, full of compassion, "I never thought of that. Wasn't it terrible?"

She didn't answer. She got up from the chair and stood behind me. I didn't know what she was going to do. She kneeled down behind me, put her arms over my shoulders and held the wooden flute before me. The sun on the varnish made it look like gold.

"Want to learn?" she asked me quietly, guiding my fingers on the instrument.

A Hundred Suits from Russia

I must get away, he thought, *just for an hour. I can't do any work here. My mother and my grandfather are too much. There's always some crisis. I can't sit down at my typewriter.* Yesterday, his grandfather had stood naked in the upstairs hall and defecated on the carpet. He had forgotten where the toilet was. Then he wiped himself with the curtain and wept, "Oy vey, vey, vey."

His mother was hysterical. "Oh, Papa, Papa, what are you doing to me?"

"Where is the toilet?" screamed the old man.

"Papa, Papa," cried his mother. "He's crazy. He's not my father. This isn't my father," and in the same breath, "My sister, the rotter, I should be as sick as she is. What have I got now?"

Her son had said, "We've got to put him away, Mother. A house is no place for him. He needs special attention."

"Put him away? Put my father away? I should put my father away? A great man, I should put away?" She was indignant. "People came from miles to hear him speak. Papa, Papa, don't step in it, oh, God, he's stepping in it, he's killing my house. Get the *javel*."

The *javel* didn't work. The house still smelt foul. But now, at least, the house was quiet. His mother and grandfather were sleeping. They had screamed at each other all night after the old man had accused his daughter of stealing all his suits. The young man crept out of his room and almost made the stairs, but his grandfather opened his door and gestured to him to come over.

"My dear son," he began, as if he were addressing a congregation, "God knows you for a fine man and, also, we should be so happy, for a poet. You must help your old grandfather who is very old and very sick and who, by his nature, has never done evil to any man in the whole world."

"Yes, Grampa, what do you want?" he asked tenderly.

"What I want?" puzzled the old man.

"You called me over. Do you want to tell me something?"

"Tell? What can an old man tell?"

"You were going," the young man said, "to ask me for some kind of help."

His mother opened the door of her room.

"What is he doing now?"

"My suits!" screamed the old man suddenly. "I came from Russia with a hundred suits. You are thieves and murderers!"

His mother's voice was strained.

"Papa, go into your room. You must sleep."

"Thieves and murderers," he continued, "my own daughter and my poor dear grandson, thieves and murderers. Suits out of my cupboard, a hundred suits from Russia!"

The young man started to descend the stairs. His mother demanded: "Where are you going?"

"Out," he cried, hating his house now and all the chaos in it. "I'm not going to stay here and listen to any more of this madness. I can't do any work here. The only thing I hear is you two people screaming at each other. I don't know which of you should be put away."

"Out," repeated his mother, nodding her head with mock understanding. "At a time like this, out. When he's needed, out. Too sensitive for life so he's not going to stay."

Controlling himself, he said, "I can't work here, do you understand? I can't work here."

"Work," his mother mocked, "fine work. In his room all day, listening to records. A poet? A deserter."

"Shut up," he cried furiously. "Shut up."

"'Shut up,'" repeated his mother. "Do you hear that, Papa? 'Shut up.' That's the way a son talks to his mother. A great man doesn't talk like that to his mother. Like your aunt, go on, leave me to do everything."

"For Christ's sake," he defended himself, "why are you making something out of this for. I want to go out for an hour. Is that so terrible?"

Then the old man, as if he were a participant in a friendly discussion, quietly inserted, "In the middle of the night they go to my closet. And now, I am left with nothing." He walked a few steps down the hall toward the bathroom, his pajama bottoms falling around his knees. "A very bad position," he muttered.

"Papa, Papa," she cried. "For a daughter to see a father like this. I would rather kill myself. *What are you doing?*"

The old man was urinating. "Get away!" he screamed at his daughter.

"My carpet, my beautiful carpet! Stop it, Papa, stop it, please, stop it. Help me!" she called to her son.

"Get away!" commanded the old man. "Thieves and murderers. Who are you talking to? Do you think I'm Shmeryl Beryl from the street? I had pupils. A hundred boys."

The young man guided his grandfather into the bathroom. He threw a towel on the pool on the carpet.

"Thank you, my dear grandson. A hundred boys like you I had."

He cleaned the carpet with *javel* and warm water. His mother leaned against a wall, weeping.

"He doesn't even know to cover himself before people, my poor papa. It's got so bad. What she did to me, my sister."

Her son said, "You know what the doctor said: that we don't have the facilities he needs, that it can only get worse. We have to see about placing him somewhere. It's the only way."

"I never knew it would get so bad," she said. "Look at the carpet. Some job. Thank you."

"The doctor said he thought he could get him into the Home," he said.

"Of course, they want him," she said. "A man like that. A Talmudist."

Her son said with sudden fury: "What are you talking about? A Talmudist. Why don't you face this? He's crazy. Your father is crazy, mentally ill, senile dementia. It's sad, but you've got to stop fooling yourself. A Talmudist. He doesn't recognize us half the time."

"She knew this, my sister," she said bitterly, "she knew all this."

"Will you forget your goddamn sister? This is your problem."

"You think it's easy," she said pathetically. "To put your own father away."

He took her hand. "It's not easy. He's sick, though. It will be better for him."

"I'll phone tomorrow," she said, defeated.

"Today."

He was sorry, but he had to be ruthless. If his mother were a different kind of person, perhaps she could spend the rest of her

life watching and caring for the old man. But it was killing her.
He had never seen her look so old.

"You've got to, Mother, you're sick yourself."

"What time is it?" asked the old man, wearing only his
pajama top.

"Two o'clock, Grampa."

He fingered his pajama top as though it were a vest.

"Where is it?" he asked slyly. "Where is my gold watch?"

"Today, Mother," he said, "it's got to be today."

"Ha. Pretend you know nothing. Look at the angels." Then
he added fiercely: "With my suits."

"Please, Papa," she pleaded, "you had no suits and you have
no gold watch."

"Mother," he said with anger, "Why are you trying to reason
with him? He doesn't understand anything you say."

"Police!" shouted the old man. "*Police!*"

"Oh, Papa." She rushed to him and embraced him. The old
man stood surprised and silent. She wept into his scattered white
hair. "Alright," she said quietly. "I'll phone today."

"Now," the young man demanded.

"Not now. When you're out."

He understood that. She needed the privacy.

"It's best for everyone," he said, descending the stairs.

He walked out on the street. The neighborhood was changing. Mostly Germans and Hungarians now. The Jews were moving
West. Westward, where the young doctors and accountants bore
their families. It was all a matter of money, he thought. With money,
my mother could keep her father, with a big house and a trained
attendant. And he felt guilty for his poems and his outrageous
ambitions and the money he wasn't bringing in. And now, they
were eating into the small capital his father had left them. I'll get

a job, he promised. I'll try again. An hour later, he returned to his house. His mother and his grandfather were sitting in the kitchen, drinking glasses of tea.

"Is it cold?" asked his mother.

"Getting. Did you call the Home?"

She started to answer, but the old man started to sing. He put down his tea and leaned back and hummed a beautiful tune without words and without personal misery, but filled with love, age, and innocence. *It's beautiful*, the young man thought. *It's more beautiful than anything I'll ever write.* He sat down beside the old man and touched his glass of tea for the warmth. He wished that this moment, in the warm kitchen with his mother and his grandfather, and the melody and the tea, and the beautiful bond of blood, would never end. His mother began to speak very rapidly.

"Do you know what he said when you were gone? That he was going to be quiet so that you could write, that one day you would be a great writer, that all the world would know. He said that people would come from miles to hear you speak."

He turned away from his mother. He knew now that his grandfather would never leave the house. The song continued, and he went over the words of his mother's poor lie.

His mother said, "And he's so happy here."

The song ended abruptly. The old man hooked his thumbs into the armholes of his vest and looked suspiciously at his audience. He folded his arms and raised his chin, superior, the master of intrigue, the banker of an underground conspiracy. Then banging his fist on the table seven times, one for each syllable, he instructed them:

"ONE HUN-DRED SUITS FROM RUS-SIA!"

Ceremonies

I suppose I will never lead the ordered life my father led. And I'll never live in the kind of house he lived in, with its rituals, its dignity, the smell of polish. Whenever I blow into Montreal, I manage to take a look at the old house. It's that large Tudor-style at the bottom of Belmont Avenue, right beside the park. It looks the same. Maybe the elms on the front lawn are taller, but they were always monumental to me. I couldn't hold on to the place or the factory and properties that went with it. A man has to discover his own responsibilities. They aren't necessarily the ones he inherits. But that's another story.

My father died when I was nine. My sister was thirteen. He had been in the hospital since the end of the summer. Now, it was the middle of January, a deep snow over the city. Nursie told us the news. She was seated solemnly at the breakfast table, her hands folded on the white cloth before her, like a schoolgirl. She greeted us good morning, but she did not speak again during the meal. She looked at us, like she did when we practised our scales, severe, but hopeful as we for a clean run. When we were finished, the door to the kitchen was mysteriously closed. The maid did not come in to remove the dishes.

"You won't be going to school this morning," she said, as we were getting up from the table. "Your poor father went very late last night. Mother is still sleeping, so we must be quiet."

"You mean he's dead, our father's dead?" asked my sister, wide-eyed.

"The funeral will be tomorrow."

We both rushed to her.

"I wanted you to eat your breakfast first."

Then the day dawned on me.

"But it can't be tomorrow, Nursie. It's my sister's birthday."

So, my sister has a quiet birthday every year. I try to remember to send a card. None of us wished her happy birthday the next morning. I looked in the large dictionary for another word for happy, but I couldn't find anything you could say on the day of a funeral. At about nine o'clock, six men entered the house and set the coffin down in the big living room. It was surprisingly huge, made of dark-grained wood, brass-handled. It made the living room more formal than we had ever known it. The men placed it on a stand and began to open the cabinet-like cover.

"Close it!" my sister cried. "Make them close it!"

In some houses, the coffin is left open hours before the ceremony. But we were afraid to see our father dead in his own living room, beside the chesterfield on which he always slept after Sunday dinner. My mother came in and told them to close it. I had turned my head and was listening for the click of the cover, but I heard nothing. These men, who make their living among the bereaved, moved noiselessly and they were gone when I opened my eyes. All the morning, my sister and I avoided that room. The mirrors of the house were soaped. It was as if the glass had suddenly become victim to a strange indoor frost. My mother stayed alone in her room. Around noon, people began to congregate in the street and in the hall of our house. An hour later, the three of us came down the stairs. The hazy winter sun glimmered on my mother's black stockings and gave, to the mourners in the doorway, a golden outline. We stood closest to the coffin, the family behind us. Friends and workers from the factory thronged the hall, the path, and the street. My uncles stood behind me in their black suits, tall and serious, occasionally touching my shoulder with manicured hands. I wore a black swatch on my sleeve and throughout the ceremony I felt for it frequently to assure myself it was still there.

"We've got to be like soldiers," whispered one of my uncles.

My sister and I were defeated. The coffin was opened. I glanced at my sister. We forced ourselves to look at him. He was swaddled in silk, wrapped in a silvered prayer shawl. His moustache was fierce and black against his white face. He appeared annoyed as if he were about to awaken, climb out of the ornate box, and resume his sleep on the more comfortable chesterfield. Throughout the prayers, we watched him. He was buried in the white cemetery close to the gates which one of our cousins donated. The gravediggers looked irreverently informal in their working clothes. A mat of artificial grass had been spread over the heaps of exhumed frozen mud. The coffin went down in a system of pullies. After the burial, there was a lighthearted atmosphere back at the house. Bagels and hard-boiled eggs were served. My uncles joked with friends of the family. My father was hardly mentioned. Though I resented the joviality, I took part in it. I looked under my great-uncle's beard and asked him why he didn't wear a tie. Then one of my uncles took me aside. He told me that now I was the man of the house, that the women were my responsibility. This made me proud. I felt like the consecrated young prince of some folk-beloved dynasty. I was the oldest son of the oldest son. It's strange, considering how far I've gone from them, that I still feel like that prince sometimes. The family left last. My aunts helped the maid collect the teacups and the small plates flecked with crumbs and caraway seeds. My mother had used the dishes with the gold pattern, thin ones you could see candlelight through. Nursie supervised the kitchen clean-up, telling my mother to get some rest. On top of the icebox, there was a vase of yellow chrysanthemums. From one of the stalks hung a black-edged card. It was from a Christian friend who did not know that flowers are not displayed in a Jewish house of mourning. Nursie was going to take them to her father's house. The flowers made me remember my sister's birthday. There hadn't been a mention of it all day. Nothing happened. I didn't devise some sweet gesture to break the silence. I didn't take a single chrysanthemum to give her or lay on her pillow. I had to wait years before I could get that maudlin. Nothing happened but this conversation. Late that night, I met my sister in the upstairs hall. Neither of us was sleeping very well. She said to come into her room.

"Your feet are cold," she said, when I had gotten into the bed.

"So are yours."

We lay for moments in silence. There was a bright winter night beyond the window. The yards of lace curtain held some of the light.

Finally, she said, "Did you look at him?"

"Yes."

"Right at him?"

"Yes."

"So did I. He looked mad, didn't he?"

"Yes."

"And his moustache so black. Like it was done with an eyebrow pencil."

"They do that to them," I said.

"We'll never see him again."

"Don't cry."

"We'll never see him again. We should have let them keep it open this morning. We could have seen him for a whole extra morning."

"Don't cry," I told her. I think it was my best moment. "Please, it's your birthday."

Mister Euemer Episodes

One bright evening, Mister Euemer sat at the front window and watched two young boys in the street, hurling mudballs at the passing automobiles. One child, a bucket between his knees, squatted near some bushes and manufactured the weapons. He handed them dripping to a blond boy who heaved them easily into the street, always barely missing the target. Apparently, the idea was just to come close. The dark street was stained with darker explosions of mud. The blond boy, poised with uplifted arm, reminded Mister Euemer of one of the joyous figures behind Joseph in Fra Angelico's *Marriage of the Virgin*. He had leaned over his *Skira* book a long while delighting in the way the red- and yellow-robed youth seemed to turn away from the procession as if he were more interested in the grace his own body promised than the outcome of holy ceremony. The blond boy hurled his weapons with the same indifferent ease, enjoyed the sweep of his arms with the same selfish pleasure. Mister Euemer was hardly aware that the child infuriated him. He was aware only of the child's beauty. "You were as beautiful as he," an inner voice told him dimly. Mister Euemer's wife came and stood behind him, leaning her chin on his skull.

"What are they up to now?" she said, massaging the muscles in his shoulders. "Look at that one. He's obviously the leader. Look at him, will you, the arrogance. There'll be plenty of broken hearts in his wake, don't you worry."

Mister Euemer did not care for his wife's observations. He wanted to watch the boy alone. Her presence was an intrusion. The child mirrored private longings and he didn't want to share the image. Her chin was like a metal point in his brain, probing, probing. His muscles were being hurt under her vigorous kneading, but he squeezed her right hand between his shoulder and his cheek and purred, "Ohhh, that feels good."

"No one in your family ever looked that good. You aren't exactly the athletes of his world," said Mrs. Euemer, giving him an extra deep double dig with her strong thumbs, and then she walked away leaving her husband tingling and relieved.

The blond boy accepted a dripping mudball from his lieutenant and aimed it at a large yellow car. He thought he caught his eye as the boy cocked his head and let the missile fly. The throw was wild. It hit the windshield and smeared across half the glass. The car swerved wildly first to one side, and then to the other, jumped the curb where miraculously there were no cars parked and, almost gracefully, rolled on its top on the dark lawn before the apartment building. The wheels were still spinning when Mister Euemer turned his eyes from the accident to look at the saboteurs. But they had fled. The noise brought his wife to his side again.

"Well, they finally got a bull's eye, didn't they?" she mused.

"No, no," lied Mister Euemer, "they didn't fire at that one. He must have been drunk or had a heart attack. There are the police already."

"Don't be fooling. If they didn't do it, they'd be the first ones in the crowd that's gathering down there, and I can't see them anywhere."

Her argument was more than a rebuke. It dismissed him altogether. He wished she would go away. The accident was a creation of the blond boy and he resented sharing it with his wife. He decided to camouflage his interest.

"Do you think that we should report them? Who knows what they might do next."

"Don't be foolish. You could ruin their lives. Look, they've got him out. What a mess. I guess he's dead."

The crowd admitted the stretcher-bearers and the mangled man through their midst, and he was borne away in the white ambulance without a siren down the darkening street. That night, listening to the shouts and machinery of workmen removing the wreck in the street below and thinking of the beautiful blond child, Mister Euemer was enthusiastic in his lovemaking.

"Nothing like a mutilation to make you hop," joked his wife.

The next day was Saturday and the afternoon was his own. His wife was going downtown for an electrolysis treatment to have some hair removed from her back. Below, he saw his wife emerge from the building and walk toward the bus stop. A large bruise on the grass and tire marks on the sidewalk were all the traces left of the accident. Then, he saw the blond boy appear from out of the bushes and stand, hands on hips, like some tourist general revisiting a devastated area. The elevator seemed incredibly slow as it dropped him to the ground floor. Would the boy still be there? The sun gleamed in the child's hair. It even occurred to Mister Euemer to stroke the golden hair, but the desire was not so strong that it had to be disciplined.

"I know you," said Mister Euemer.

Without speaking, the boy moved a few steps away. *What grace*, thought Mister Euemer. *What makes us forget how to move like that?* "You once moved as beautifully as he," an inner voice dimly replied, giving no satisfaction.

"I do know you," repeated Mister Euemer playfully.

"Listen, Mister, I ain't inrested whether yuh know me or no. I never seen so many queers in a city, trying to pick a guy up. Lemme alone, will yuh."

Mister Euemer was surprised and shocked at the child's language and the coarseness of his voice. Well, he can't be held responsible for his upbringing, he rationalized. The blond boy did not go away. Mister Euemer thought he even detected a smile on the boy's red lips. The boy was swinging his leg like a ballet dancer, limbering up, kicking at the ruined grass.

"I suppose there was an accident here," said Mister Euemer.

"Sure, sure," mocked the child with a bored voice.

"What do you mean 'sure, sure'?" Mister Euemer was a little annoyed at the child's insolence.

"Sure, sure," in the same voice.

Down the street another child waved and called: "Hiya, Star."

Mister Euemer recognized him as the weapon-maker of the evening before.

"Is that your name, Star?"

Mister Euemer thought it was a fine name for him.

"Sure, sure. Well, so long, Mister. I gotta go now. That's my buddy."

He started away, swinging his hips in an exaggerated fashion. Mister Euemer lunged and caught his arm.

"Just a moment, Star. I do know you and I know your friend too. And I saw you throw the mudball at the yellow car and we both know what happened."

Terror spread on the boy's face, not disfiguring him but only dramatizing his beauty. Mister Euemer did not release his grip. The boy's arm seemed fragile as though he could break it if he gripped tighter.

"Whadya want from me, Mister? Yer making a mistake. Mudballs? Yer crazy."

But he knew he was caught. The truth is that Mister Euemer didn't know exactly what he wanted from the boy.

"I want—I just want to talk to you. In my apartment." Star tried to make a break. Mister Euemer countered and used his other hand to seize the boy's shoulder. "Otherwise, it's the police."

Star's friend was walking toward them.

"Tell your friend to go away."

"Beat it," Star said to the boy who had stopped a few feet away.

"Aw, Star, you with him?" He glanced scornfully at Mister Euemer. "You said you'd be with me this afternoon. There's nobody home. Gee, Star, you promised. You said to meet you here, then we'd go. . . ." Now the boy was close to tears.

"I said beat it. Now go, take off."

"O.K. Mister. Let's get outta here."

"Just cause he's going to give you money," his friend pouted, rubbing his eyes.

"Scram."

Mister Euemer held his grip until they were in the elevator. Remembering his own childhood intrigues, he wondered what the two boys were up to.

"Your friend was very disappointed, wasn't he?"

"Yeah. He likes me a lot."

And very softly, as they walked down the corridor: "I'll get even with yuh."

Mister Euemer preferred not to hear the last remark. There was no longer fright on the boy's face. They sat in the living room. Mister Euemer asked him how old he was. The boy told him thirteen.

"Oh, I thought you were younger."

"Yeah, they all do."

Mister Euemer put a silver dish of chocolates beside the boy. Star put one into his mouth after the other, finishing them all.

"Might as well get something outta this," Star muttered.

Mister Euemer no longer resented the boy's hostility. After all, he thought, I've made him change his plans for the afternoon. Mister Euemer loved to watch him eat, loved to see the red tongue discover specks of candy on the red lips. Mister Euemer showed him the picture in the *Skira* book.

"It's a dead ringer for you."

"Sure, sure."

The boy hardly glanced at the reproduction. Mister Euemer walked to the window. A funeral procession was passing in the street below, the black limousines, a shinier segment of the general traffic.

"You know, Star, I did the same sort of things as you when I was a kid. And that's not as long ago as you might think."

And then Mister Euemer began to talk quickly and passionately about his childhood. A long story of caves and secret clubs, passwords and enemies, brave adventures, ingenious pranks, and dreams, dreams, dreams. He must have talked for over an hour.

Star sat motionless in his chair, his lovely head tilted backwards, staring at the ceiling. Mister Euemer ended a sentence with a sigh.

"You're not listening, are you, Star?"

"Sure, sure. Yuh want me to get undressed now?"

"What are you talking about?"

"Yuh mean, yuh don't want me to get undressed?"

"Don't be absurd."

The boy put his hands on his face, covering his blue eyes. Then he began to laugh. Mister Euemer began to laugh, too.

"Holy Mackerel, I thought you wuz just trying to get something for nothing. I thought cuz yuh had me up a tree on accounta last night, Christ, yuh mean yuh ain't a queer?"

"Young man."

"Yuh mean, yuh got me up here just to gimme that crap about pirates and good guys?"

"I thought you might be interested," said Mister Euemer, for want of something else, suddenly ashamed.

Down on the sidewalk, he saw his wife returning from her appointment.

"Perhaps you'd better go now. I'm expecting my wife any minute."

Star did not move.

"And yuh sent my buddy away bawling, just cuz yuh wanted to sound off to me? What kinda creep are yuh, anyways?"

"Look, young man, if I've wasted your time, perhaps this will make it up to you."

He dug into his pocket and handed the boy a bill.

"Sure, it'll make it up to me, yuh creep," and he took the money.

Mister Euemer was alarmed by the hate on the boy's face.

"Now, if you don't mind leaving, my wife will—Hey, what are you doing?"

"Sure, sure, yer wife."

The blond boy was undressing, stepping out of his trousers. He flung his underwear and shirt on the floor. Even in his panic, Mister Euemer noticed the blond pubic hair.

"Stop it, stop it!" he cried.

Mister Euemer grabbed at the dancing boy. His wife opened the front door and stepped into the living room. She saw her husband struggling with a blond, naked boy. She made a wet noise in her throat, turned and ran from the apartment. Mister Euemer trembled, panicked. Then he ran after her, but she had caught the elevator before him.

"Chalk one up for me," laughed the boy, pulling on his trousers.

Mister Euemer ran after his wife in the street. When he got to her, she was weeping. He put his arm around her, and she allowed herself to be led back to the apartment.

"Please, don't get the wrong idea," he began in a pleading voice. "He played a trick on me."

But he knew she would never believe him.

The Shaving Ritual

Mister Euemer, rhymes with tumor, lay on his side of the great white bed and, with all his poor heart, hated his sleeping wife who faintly snored a warm foot away. He frankly hoped that she would choke to death with the next heave of her formless, silk-covered bosom. He even recited a short silent prayer to that effect but, before he could seal it with a silent amen, she adjusted her body suddenly and frightened him out of it. The autumn moon cast a silver eye into the modern room so full of sleep and hate. The perfectly shaven arm of his wife gleamed above the white comforter. He could not help thinking that it looked like a smooth, enchanted eel, or a scaleless snake, milky, rare, and dangerous. And the damn comforter. Oh, no, she couldn't have blankets like everyone else.

"Blankets are too bristly, they hurt," she had complained successfully a few months ago in their first week of marriage.

Then his heavy Harris Tweed suit had disappeared. He loved it because it made him look so British, even though the pants chafed his thighs.

His wife said: "You must have left it at the hotel in Bermuda."

That was impossible. He knew he couldn't have taken a tweed suit on a tropical honeymoon. Other things had disappeared.

A rabbit's foot from his key chain. The brown stag's foot letter opener from the desk. A cactus plant that one of his best friends had sent them.

"It died," she said simply.

She almost had become hysterical when he brought home the puppy.

"You can't bring that in here!"

"What do you mean? Here, take the little fellow. Just put your cheek against his—"

She pushed his hands away violently and retreated backwards into the room.

"It won't bite, darling."

She had begun to shudder, moving her hands over her breasts and shoulders as if she were washing in a shower.

"Agh agh agh," was her soft intense gurgle.

Mister Euemer, puzzled, took the innocent beast out of the house and gave it to a neighbor. His wife was perfectly composed when he returned, but she wouldn't let him kiss her until he had washed his hands.

That night, when they were lying in that tight uncomfortable embrace young lovers have for each other, she said unexpectedly, breaking the usual silence of their intimacy: "There would have been hairs over everything."

Mister Euemer stared at his wife in the moonlight. He studied her naked arm. He'd been cheated. He'd been taken in. He was the worst thing an American could be, a sucker. He surrendered himself to a flush of shame. He should have been suspicious that first night she had given herself to him, a week before the marriage ceremony. Mister Euemer had never been exactly proud of his body. He always felt inferior on the beach because of the paucity of hair on his chest and limbs. As he undressed, he saw his future wife looking at him with obvious pleasure in her devouring gaze. It filled him with delight and confidence and he loved her more than adequately.

"I'm so happy your body is smooth, not covered with hair like some kind of ape."

And he thought how kind she was, and they laughed and renewed their embraces. The Shaving Ritual (Mister Euemer capitalized it in his mind) began during the honeymoon. He was waiting for her in bed when he heard the bath running.

"Just to cool off," she called.

"I envy the water," he returned gallantly.

For a while he listened with satisfaction and anticipation to the music of her splashing.

"Can I watch you?" he petitioned at the closed door.

"All right," she agreed in a shy, proper bride's voice.

"You're very beautiful, Mrs. Euemer," he said, standing in admiration above her.

He loved the way she replied: "I try my best, Mister Euemer."

She was shaving her legs, a pleasant enough activity to observe, but there was something wrong. She was shaving her *thighs*. He was disturbed on two accounts. First of all, it struck him as unnatural. The women he had observed, and that included his sister and two loose ladies with whom he had had adventures, all the women he could remember, and he racked his brain, none of them had ever shaved above the knee. Secondly, and more important, he had come to love those orchards of tiny brown hairs on her thighs. And in as tactful a voice as possible, this is exactly what he told her. She did not try to disguise the contempt which his remark invoked in her.

"Try not to be disgusting, will you, dear," she commanded through a hard mouth.

A bridegroom's passion prevented him from recognizing the intensity of the rebuke. Nevertheless, he knew now that it had been the beginning of the end. Each night after that, before retiring, Mister Euemer listened to his wife splashing in the tub. The Ritual began to take longer and longer. Sometimes, Mister Euemer fell asleep waiting. Quite naturally, this had a bad effect on his day at the office.

"Do you have to do it every night?"

"You wouldn't ask me that if you knew anything about how fast hair grows."

She seemed almost hurt by the question. It did no good to remind her that he himself got by with shaving every second morning. A few days later, she included her arms in the Shaving Ritual. He tried to put his foot down.

"I've never heard of a woman shaving her arms. It's a beautiful thing to see a hint of down on a woman's arms. I remember how it went gold on the cruise."

"Are you trying to make me sick?" she demanded.

Her limbs were smooth as porcelain, even if stroked the wrong way, but he got fewer and fewer opportunities to stroke them. She stayed in the bath as long as three hours, drawing the silver razor back and forth over her soaped limbs. One night, he could bear it no longer. He stormed into the bathroom and seized her wrist.

"This has gone too far," he nearly shouted. "You're my lawful wife and you're coming to bed with me."

She did not resist. She rose Venus-like from the water and allowed herself to be dried briskly. In the morning, she had her revenge. He awakened horrified to see her naked before the bathroom mirror. She was shaving her face, shaving that faint, faint moustache, which he loved so much, shaving the nearly invisible brown hairs of her chin, which he had charted on his passion's map.

"Oh, my God! What are you doing?"

"You don't want to be married to the Bearded Lady, do you?"

She grinned through the lather. He couldn't find a voice to reply. He watched the razor wielded through the lather like a silver plough on a field of snow. So, the Shaving Ritual developed a morning chapter. And, in truth, Mister Euemer was not entirely disgusted with his wife's bizarre performance each a.m. He accustomed himself to it. It titillated him somewhat. It aroused him. The Shaving Ritual was his secret, deep, delicious, evil, and dangerous, a Black Mass, which he recited to himself during the working day. It filled him with that sense of superiority, which he who had debauched himself felt toward the conventional and uninitiated. He wondered if Mrs. Euemer was not an extremely clever woman, planning these devices to keep him interested and excited. He asked her to keep the door open, so he could observe the rites. He learned to wait patiently for her fragrant body, smooth from the steel, warm from the bath. Of course, he was often disturbed. Stabs of guilt tore into the glimmering fabric of pleasure. Were they wrong, were they *unhealthy*? An ugly word like *pervert* crossed his mind. But all he had to do was recall her perfect, incredible body, so carefully attended, so lovingly prepared, and the fabric restored itself in all its brightness. He came to understand that, for him, passion was a delicate balance of attraction and revulsion. He congratulated himself on his unusual distinguished sensibility. But tonight, she had gone too far. She had shaved the downy triangle where once he had laid his burning cheek. She shaved that place and insisted that he do the same.

"Your armpits, too," she added firmly.

She had upset the delicate balance. He protested vigorously. He would do no such thing. Even the suggestion was humiliating. He thought of eunuchs and castratos and appendicitis patients. Hair was the history-old mark of manhood. He didn't care what she did with hers but, by Jesus, he was keeping his.

"Very well," she replied, with that sound of contempt the pure have for the impure, whatever words they use. "Just refrain from handling me until you revise your opinions."

She checked his inquiring hand by tugging the sheets and comforter around her body, armoring herself in a silk and linen cocoon. Mister Euemer, rhymes with tumor, lay on his side of the great white bed and, with all his poor heart, hated his sleeping wife who faintly snored a warm foot away. He wondered when she would discover the tiny hairs in her nostrils and how she would eliminate them. She wasn't snoring now, how could he have thought she ever snored? He studied her body in the moonlight. Her bosom wasn't formless at all. He watched her and imperceptibly, as the moon moves, his feelings moved from hatred into passion, from disgust and outrage into a desperate need for the enjoyment and possession of her. He peeled away the bedclothes. She awakened for a moment, he caught the glare in her eyes and she gathered the bedclothes angrily to repair the cocoon around herself. It was something more than instinct and less than thought that catapulted him out of the bed toward the bathroom. He threw off his pajamas, turned on the shower, grabbed his razor and pressurized lather, and stepped under the water.

"If that's what she wants, what difference does it make to me?" he muttered to himself.

He aimed and squirted the thick cream over his body and began to apply the razor, his mind still lost with the sleeping woman in the next room. Then he saw naked Mrs. Euemer beside the sink. She was putting a new blade in her razor. She stepped into the shower with him and went to work under his left arm. Soon, they were laughing and kissing and singing. Both were covered with soap and they were drawing their razors over each other. In their joy, they were careless, and their bodies were soon bleeding from dozens of small painless slashes. They squirted and slashed and hugged and, when they finally turned off the water and sank to the gleaming bottom of the porcelain tub in a sexual embrace, they looked like crazy writhing barber poles.

"You are so beautiful," she moaned, "and so good to me."

He buried his face in her fragrant, dripping hair. The tiny cuts on his shoulders were beginning to sting, not that it mattered.

Lullaby

Mister Euemer saw himself the father of many sons, the Moses of a new tribe, the almost barbaric founder of a proud dynasty. "My seed will be spread over the earth," he proclaimed in the booming chambers of his imagination. In the warm hovels of his heart, his sons kneeled for the paternal benediction. His wife had told him she was pregnant. He stood naked before the bathroom mirror and marvelled at his loins. He swelled his chest and pretended to orate. There was no one in the bathroom, but Mister Euemer and dreams of progeny. His wife pregnant! He thought of melons swelling in the sun, of trees laden with heavy fruit, of bubbling swamps, of warm oceans, of all that is ripe and lush and brings forth life. And he had done it. Mister Euemer. Mister Julius Caesar Alexander Genghis Leviathan Euemer. What if the baby should die? In the crib. Not a week old. Oh, the tiny coffin and oh, the yearly visits to the cemetery, and oh, the light of blue flowers. Or what if the baby were stolen? By the gypsies. By an eagle. By kidnappers. Oh, the recriminations and oh, the ransom and oh, the television appeal to the nation. Mister Euemer fairly gleamed as his imagination soared above the silver faucets and shower tiles.

"How long are you going to be in there?" demanded his wife from the bedroom. "I've got to get into the bath. I'm filthy."

Mister Euemer did not cover himself with the Turkish towel. Tonight, he was supreme.

"C'mon in," he sang.

"Aren't you cold?" She drew her bath.

Mister Euemer watched his wife as she bathed. He gave her stomach special attention. He loved her. This was the woman he had fertilized. His wife. His woman.

"You're a perfect ass, standing there."

Then his wife did a strange thing. She didn't shave. She, who every night ran her razor over her legs and armpits and other secret fields. She, who hated body hair with a venom and wielded a sharp razor in a religious war against it. She, who kept her flesh like a statue's flesh, but soft as a swan. She didn't shave.

"Do you want me to change your blade, dear?" he inquired helpfully.

"No. I think I'll let it go for tonight."

She let it go for the next night too. And the night after that. In fact, she stopped shaving altogether. Her legs tickled Mister Euemer. She became hairier as her belly swelled. The faint moustache on her upper lip, which previously she had so carefully doctored, now became quite noticeable. Mister Euemer didn't mind. He had learned to love his wife and his wife's pleasures. And Mrs. Euemer seemed to be taking enormous pleasure in the new bristling orchards of hair now growing free on her body, once so smooth and carefully guarded. It was as though as her body nourished the forming child in her womb, she took pains to nourish the growing product of her skin. She was the complete mother and whatever she brought forth was important and valuable. Because of her new interest, Mister Euemer even thought of growing a beard. But that was hopeless on two accounts. He could never get away with it at the office, and he only had to shave three times a week anyway, which indicated how little hair he had in the first place. Mrs. Euemer grew into a shaggy mountain of life. She spent hours admiring her exaggerated anatomy, balancing her heavy breasts, the instruments of sustenance, massaging her great belly, the house of life. She strutted. She waddled. She crowed. At first, Mister Euemer shared in her praise. He even called her Great Mother for a joke.

"Sometimes, Great Mother, I think we should make you a human sacrifice to appease you and win your favor."

And in her fertile glory, Mrs. Euemer did not think this suggestion entirely outrageous. But she began to neglect herself. At least, Mister Euemer thought so. She never seemed to comb her hair. She molded it carelessly into shape and secured it with a forest of hairpins. There were hairpins all over the apartment. He stepped on them and slept on them. Wisps of hair unfastened themselves and much of the time she looked like a suburban Medusa. She bathed too seldom. Sometimes, he thought she wasn't brushing her teeth. Often, when he came home from work, the beds were not yet made. And she grew, grew, grew. Her moustache became blacker, her hair more fiercely undone. Hair appeared on her body where he would never have suspected. Her breasts went beyond attractive movie proportions. Her belly was enormous. Mister Euemer looked closely at pregnant women he saw in the street. And he had never so many times before. He was sure they weren't so large as his wife. It appeared to him that his wife was trying to grow herself into the apartment, trying to expand herself to fill the four corners. He suggested to her that perhaps she was becoming a little careless in regard to her personal hygiene.

She replied, closing the conversation, "There are certain eccentricities which a pregnant woman is usually forgiven. I don't ask for pickles at midnight, etc. I just get a little primitive, I suppose."

Mister Euemer no longer marvelled at his loins in the bathroom mirror. He no longer prefaced his name with the titles of conquerors. He knew who the conquerors and creators of this world were. And they weren't men. The apartment was dirty. The ashtrays and wastebaskets were full. She couldn't bring herself to get rid of anything. When Mrs. Euemer came tumbling into bed each night, like a glacier breaking into the ocean, Mister Euemer experienced a feeling he could not identify. It was fear. But as Mrs. Euemer approached her time, suddenly everything changed. He came home one evening to find the apartment tidy, the bathroom gleaming, the black wriggles of hairpins nowhere in evidence. Mrs. Euemer was herself transformed. She was groomed and powdered. That night, he discovered her body was as smooth as always. And she no longer had a superior, luxurious air about her. Her face no longer wore that benevolent, almost obscene, expression that seemed to proclaim that the earth's navel siphoned her abundant juices for sustenance. She was no more the Great Mother.

"I looked in the mirror and got tired of being a slob," she said to her husband, who lay beside her between the fresh sheets.

But this was not altogether true. And there was a little sadness in her voice. Mister Euemer took his wife's hand. He squeezed it tenderly. Again, he saw himself the father of sons. But no hero now, no barbaric progenitor. A simple man, in a simple house. Married to a good wife. A teller of stories. A pal to his children. A member of the community. Dad. He kissed her cheek and tasted salt. She was crying silently.

"What is the matter?" he asked her softly.

After a silence she told him, her telling a flood of confession, "I only realized today what was happening to me. I'm going to have a child. A child. Do you know what that means? It means that I'm a mother. Not for a week or a month, but forever and ever. It's like everything has been set down for me and nothing can change it now. A mother with children and that's it. A decree. And I'm young. Look at me. I'm young and I've never been anywhere, never done anything and now it's all over."

Into the night, she wept for the youth she thought she had been cheated out of, and for the spires, towers, canals, and hills, she thought she would never see, and she wept secretly for the romances in obscure village inns which she would never enjoy. Mister Euemer lay dwarfed beside her and tried to comfort her, but she cried herself to sleep. He felt tender and protective, and adjusted the white bedclothes over her huge form. He knew that all pregnant women underwent such doubts and he felt himself deep in the role of Understanding Husband. He held her hand far into his sleep.

The next morning, he saw her contorting her body beside the closet. She was trying to struggle into one of her normal sized dresses. It was a hopeless battle and soon she discarded the twisted garment in a corner. "Vanity, vanity," smiled Mister Euemer. But when he came home that evening, she was in the hall leaning dangerously over the stairwell. Mister Euemer was alarmed. His wife was gasping when he got to her. She had somehow compressed herself into her old clothes and could hardly breathe. He took her into the apartment and undressed her. There were seam marks in her flesh. They weren't too deep, so he knew she couldn't have been like this for too long. She breathed heavily on the bed and the breathing became sobbing.

"I don't want it. I don't want it."

"Easy, easy," chanted Mister Euemer.

She snuggled clumsily beside him and allowed him to comfort her. Mister Euemer loved to hold his wife. He did not understand her despair. Locked in their embrace, they were like a grotesque Janus statue, each face staring toward a different conclusion. Both faced with the reality of living together, both were facing the other way. In his mind, dimly, "A child will bind her to me forever." In her mind, dimly, "A child will make me ugly and used forever." Did either of them know that a man needs to be sure of his woman, that a woman needs to be sure of her innocence? Certainly, they had read it somewhere. Mister Euemer dreamed of Germans impaling babies on their bayonets. The dream was interrupted by a cry of pain from his wife. It was time. He called the doctor and a taxi and then he dressed her. She said nothing, and her lips were white. In the taxi he noticed that her fists were clenched.

"Everything will be all right," he whispered.

She shut her eyes and shook her head. Only once did she speak, "I hate it."

Mister Euemer sat in the waiting room. He was trembling. On another floor, his wife was being delivered of her baby. Suddenly, he was overwhelmed by fear, terror on behalf of the new child, so new, so frail. He couldn't bear to be so far from the act of birth. It was his first experience of pure paternal concern. Softly, he left the waiting room. There were two interns in the corridor. He walked past them quickly and climbed three flights of stairs. Between him and the operating room sat a nurse at a desk.

"They sent for me," he lied to her, in a solemn voice.

She nodded as he passed. As he approached, the doctor emerged from the operating room. He laid one of his hands on Mister Euemer's right shoulder.

"I was just going to send for you. Your wife is in good condition, but I'm afraid the baby is stillborn. Depending on your religious preference, we will . . . ."

They were wheeling his wife out of the operating room. Her eyes were closed but there was a faint smile on her lips. A smile of satisfaction. The sight was altogether hideous to Mister Euemer.

"She did it," he screamed, "she did it purposely."

He burst into the white operating room.

"Where is it? Where is my child?"

Two surprised interns looked up from a cloth crib-like contraption. Mister Euemer lunged between them and swept up the dead baby. Then he fled, tipping over an instrument tray.

"The Angel of Death," joked one of the interns.

"Stop him, stop him," echoed down the corridor.

Mister Euemer ran downstairs, through doors, skidded around a corner, crossed a short hall, opened another door and sank to the floor in a dark closet, among mops and pails, smelling of *javel* water, the baby cradled in his arms. There was so much he wanted to tell the child. There was so much he must be made to understand. War and music and hunger and love. Good luck and bad luck. Years of weather and walking and living. The whole universe of knowledge and feeling. He must impart everything to the child. The responsibility was huge, crushing. Would he have time?

Lullabies and myths crowded his mind and he thought he spoke them to his baby, whom he rocked in his arms, but all his voice said was, "Be careful, be careful, be careful, be careful," over and over.

An hour later a charwoman opened the closet and screamed. Mister Euemer awakened and stood up slowly. He had trouble rising because he still cradled the baby. Very gently he handed the baby to the astonished woman.

"Be careful," he whispered and then walked blindly down the corridor.

They took him to his wife. He climbed on the hospital bed and lay beside her. He was not sure which of them was weeping. She was all he had in this world. She held his face in her hands and told him that they must love one another.

"I love you, oh, I love you," he said.

And beside this sincere and solemn declaration, an absurd thought fluttered: that his wife liked the scent of *javel* water which clung to his clothes. For which he must be forgiven.

A Week is a Very Long Time

They leaned out of their small high window, squashing shoulders, looking at the street below. Staircases plunged into the street like rusted needles in a narrow pincushion. Bulging ashcans sentried the dirty sidewalk. It was early morning. A few tired cats cruised the gutters and walls for a sleeping hole. A blue mist lightly lay on the flesh-colored buildings like a scarf on an underwater body, ready to be whipped away by the wind and the emerging sun. The traffic was being let out of its sheds and garages, herds forming at intersections under the slow lights, and most alarm clocks were ready to spring in another half-hour. They had hardly been out of bed for the last five days. Even with the small window wide open, all the air in their room smelled like the bed, smelled like her, smelled like him. He rubbed his bristled chin on her white shoulder, still too beautiful to be familiar, and with her arm she half-circled his naked waist. Her arm, her wrist, were so delicate that he imagined them clinging to his back like an unweaned creature to its mother. They had spent all their money on the rent and the little food which they had already eaten.

"Cold?" he asked.

"No. It feels good," she said, smiling.

"Hungry?" he asked.

"Maybe a little. You?"

He laughed. "Wouldn't refuse it if it was set in front of me."

"Well, don't worry about that," she said. "We shouldn't have bought such expensive stuff, like the paté and the anchovies."

"What the hell," he said, meaning it wasn't every day.

"I suppose so. Where are you going?"

Her shoulder felt cold without his pressed against it. He was looking under the bed for the cigarettes. "God, it's filthy under here," he said, without any surprise.

"What do you expect for eight dollars a week?" she said.

He stood up and stretched. "We've still got two more days. We agreed on a week," he reminded her.

"I didn't say anything. I'd like to stay for a year." She stretched. "Stretching is like yawning, it's contagious."

"Stay here with no food?" he asked, searching the bedclothes.

"We would get food," she said. Her voice was a little too serious for his liking. "We could work," she added.

"Sure," he said, "only it's called marriage. That wasn't part of the agreement. Hey, who put the cigarettes under the pillow? They're a mess."

He straightened one out and presented it to her.

"You put them there," she said.

"Why me?" he declared with mock injury.

"You had them last," she said, ready to prove it.

He lit her cigarette and she blew a mouthful of smoke into the morning.

She said, "I love smoking with nothing on."

He kissed the nape of her neck and they resumed their idle

watch in the window. Across the street, an old man in an oversized raincoat stood in a doorway, pressed against the door as if he were hiding.

"Why do you like smoking with nothing on?" he asked like a straight man.

"It's so—so luxurious."

She shivered over the word and he put his arm across her shoulders. The little man on the other side leaned forward, looked up and down the street, and satisfied that it was empty, gathered the folds of his raincoat around him like a cape and stepped onto the sidewalk.

"It's been a good week," he yawned.

He flicked a roll of ashes out of the window and watched it fall like a feather for a moment and then disintegrate in the rising wind.

She closed her eyes against his arm. "Oh, it's been a beautiful week."

He said, "You're beautiful."

She said, "Will we ever do this again?"

He held her tighter. "Maybe," he said.

"Will we?" she persisted in a schoolgirl's voice, which was authentic and almost pleading.

"Maybe you're too beautiful," he said, because he didn't want to say anything else. The wind moved in her hair, detaching and floating a wisp.

He said, "Maybe you won't want to or maybe I won't want to."

The old man in the swaddling coat kneeled and peered under a parked car, then he got up and brushed his knees, looking around him. The lovers watched him idly as people watch moving water.

"I know I will want to," she replied. "Will you?"

"Don't be so sure," he said. "You haven't had time to think about it. Wait till you get outside."

"I have thought, and I am sure," she persisted. "What about you?"

He said, "Let's not talk so much. I think we agreed not to talk too much."

"We agreed on lots of things before we came here," and she added in a softer voice, "but things change when you live with somebody for a time."

He withdrew his arm from her shoulder and squeezed it between them. He dropped the butt and it turned in its fall like a tiny doomed parachutist.

"I don't want things to change," he said severely. "We met, and we decided to do this because we wanted to, no strings attached. That was the whole point."

She knew he was annoyed but still she was compelled to probe him. "What will you do after, go back to your job?"

"Probably," he said, "or get another one. You?"

"The same," she said, and after a pause, "Won't you want to see me again? I don't necessarily mean like this, just to be friends?"

He said with aggravated patience, "Think back to our agreement. We'll do what we feel like doing: If we want to, we will, if we don't want to, we won't."

"I'll want to," she said.

"Fine. Now let's not talk so much."

The sun jelled suddenly between two buildings, intensely blackening the charade of chimneys, dissolving the scarves of blue mist. Across the street, the old man peered under another parked car, didn't find what he was looking for, and returned to his doorway. Down the street, someone got into his car and drove away. A cat appeared a few feet from where the old man was waiting and crossed in front of him, proud, starved, and muscular. With a flurry of folds, the old man leaped after the animal. Effortlessly, the cat changed its direction and swiftly padded down stoned stairs to a cellar entrance. The man coughed and followed, stopped, baffled, and climbed to the street empty-handed. Although the lovers had idly watched the scene, they didn't remark on it to each other.

"What's the matter?" he asked her. "You've got gooseflesh."

"Nothing," she said.

"Cold? We can close the window," he offered.

"No thanks," she said.

"Want another cigarette? Still a few left."

"No," she said, "they're all crushed. There are holes in the paper, you can't draw."

"You put your fingers over the hole, like a flute, and they draw okay," he said.

"No, thank you."

She refastened a wisp of floating hair. He studied her fingers in their exercise, knowing how perfect they were.

"Well," he said, "come on, what's the matter? There's not talking and there's not talking. You're too quiet."

"I was wondering," she said.

"About what?" he asked.

"About you," she said.

"What about me?"

"You won't want to hear," she said.

"What won't I want to hear?" he asked.

"What I was wondering," she said smiling.

"Look," he said, "Will you stop this merry-go-round and say what you want to."

She spoke very softly, "I was wondering if there have been other girls like me, but I know the answer."

"I thought that was what you were wondering," he said, not without kindness.

"Then why did you ask me?" Her eyes became misty. Very softly, she said like a good schoolgirl, "Not to ask was part of the agreement."

He took her in his arms, their bodies smooth and cool from the morning wind. *She is beautiful*, he thought. *Why can't she leave it alone?* He felt the warm tiny rivulet of a tear on his shoulder.

"Please, don't cry," he said.

"I don't want to," she wept openly.

In the street, the old man with the flowing coat was lying on his stomach under the bumper of a car, grasping after a cat he had managed to corner between the curb and the wheel. He was kicking his feet in the excitement, trying to get the cat by the hind legs, getting scratched and nipped. He finally succeeded, extracted the cat from the shadows and held it above his head, where it wriggled and convulsed like a pennant in a violent wind. The squeals of the animal brought the attention of the lovers.

"My God," she exclaimed, "what's he doing with that cat?"

They forgot their embrace and leaned out of the window. The old man staggered under the desperate struggle of the animal, his face buried in his chest, away from the thrashing claws. He regained his footing and wielding the cat like an axe, he brought it in a downward and hard against the sidewalk, his coat billowing. They heard the head smash from their window. The cat convulsed like a landed fish.

She turned her head away. "What's he doing now?" she wanted to be told.

"He's putting it in a bag," he said.

The old man, kneeling beside the twitching cat, had produced a paper bag from out of his swaddling and was attempting to stuff the cat into it. As he fumbled, he looked about furtively.

"I'm sick," she said. She joined her hands behind his back, hiding her face against his chest. "Can't you do something?"

Then it occurred to him that he could do something.

"Hey, you!" he shouted down, "what do you think you're doing?"

The old man stood up suddenly, trying to identify the source of the voice.

"Yes, I mean you!" he shouted from his window.

The old man froze, looking down at his slaughter, he was uncertain whether to grab it and run, or just run. He vibrated his hands in terrible indecision and then he fled down the street coughing and empty-handed, his coat gathered as though he were a girl crossing a stream.

She gurgled, "I'm going to be sick," she managed, breaking from him to the sink. She leaned over the sink and then she lay on the bed breathing hard. "That was close," she said, "I thought I was going to be sick."

He sat beside her. "You're shivering. I'll close the window."

"All right," she said.

"Can I get you something?" he asked.

"Just lie beside me," she said.

He lay beside her, stroking her face.

"How do you feel now?" he asked.

"Better," she said. "What a terrible thing to see."

He agreed with her, then he said, "Maybe I shouldn't have frightened him off."

"Why?" she asked.

"I'll tell you later," he said.

"What do you mean?" she asked.

"When you feel better," he said.

"I'm alright," she said, "tell me now."

He said, "Maybe he was starving, the old man. Maybe he won't eat today."

"A cat?" she said, unbelieving.

"When you're starving. He was there all the time we were in the window, he was looking for something. That's what he was looking for. Probably been there all night."

"Oh, how terrible," she said.

She held him tightly. It was not the kind of embrace they had agreed on, to be enjoyed with an appetite and forgotten like a meal.

"You're upset," he said. "You're tired, we didn't sleep very much. Try to sleep now."

"Will you sleep too?" she asked.

"Yes," he said, "we're both tired."

With his hand he smoothed her face and hair, grazed her closed eyelids. He remembered the miniature work of the wind, unfastening and floating wisps and locks. He remembered the first days of their week, the strength of her limbs, the honesty of their hunger. A week is a long time. It was always like that in the beginning, it was always like this in the end.

"What will he do now?" she said.

"I don't know," he said. "Stand in another doorway. He'll probably have to wait for tonight. There are too many people in the street now."

She said, "Now I'm sort of sorry too. Him, in that ridiculous coat."

"Yes," he said. "Try to sleep."

She kept her eyes closed. She opened her mouth and her lips trembled.

"Don't say it," he cried silently. "If you say it, everything will become impossible."

Then she said simply, "I love you."

"I . . ."

But he could not reply, he could never reply to it. It was far too late to mention the agreement.

"You don't have to say anything," she said. "I wanted to tell you."

"Thank you," he said. "I . . ."

"Will you kiss me?" she asked quietly.

He kissed her mouth lightly.

"Damn you," he cried silently. "Damn your beauty, damn your gentleness, damn the old man, damn the murdered cat."

"Are you angry with me?" she said.

"What do you mean?" he said.

"For what I said."

He told her no.

"Are you happy?" she asked.

"Yes," he said.

"I'm happy I told you," she said.

"Try to sleep," he told her.

"I can sleep now," she said.

She adjusted her position and moved closer to him, not for sensation, but for warmth and protection. He held her lightly, no mistress now, but a refugee child, bereaved. As her breathing grew regular, his panic flourished. It seized him, heating the room like an oven, drawing the sweat on his palms. Now she was asleep. Yes, he was sure she was asleep. Carefully, he disengaged himself from her hold, extracted himself from the tangled sheets. If only she wasn't so beautiful. How could he leave her? He dressed like a thief, his skin screeching against the fabric, his shirt uncrumpling like a paper bag. She didn't awaken. His hands fumbled. All he had left was change. He put half of it on the dresser. She loves to smoke with nothing on. He sorted out and left her the best cigarettes. Why did she have to say it? He wasn't going to get himself into anything, damn it, damn it.

A round sun burned above the buildings. All the parked cars had been driven away. A few janitors, brooms in hand, stood blinking among the garbage cans watching the downtown traffic as it stopped and gathered, started and spread. He ran into the street, the fragrance of her flesh trapped in his clothes. The sun, the fresh air, startled him and he stopped for several deep breaths.

"Morning," said a janitor. "Nice day."

"Beautiful," he said, feeling suddenly a new man in a new society.

"Y'know, they should never give them cars, the way they drive."

"I suppose not," he replied, ready to agree with everything, loving the day.

"Drunk most of the time," said the janitor. "Just out of the trees. I had a few in my building. Filth? I said to them—"

They heard a frantic woman's voice.

The janitor looked up and said, "Ain't that from your room, your missus? Hey, where you running?"

He picked his way through the traffic to the other side. He thought he could make out what she was saying. There was the mutilated cat half in the paper bag, the old man's meal. People were walking past it, giving it an occasional curious glance and plenty of berth on their walk to work. He ran like a football player between the crowds until, two blocks away, he knocked someone down and stopped to help her up.

The Jukebox Heart

Excerpt from a Journal

When I was about thirteen years old, I did the things my friends did until they went to bed, then I'd walk miles along Ste. Catherine Street, a night lover, peeking into marble tabled cafeterias where men wore overcoats even in the summer, stopping for intense minutes in front of novelty shops to catalogue the magic and tricks, rubber cockroaches, handshake buzzers, explosive cigars, and leaking glasses, sometimes choosing a sexy pipe for my future manhood from among the terraces of briar in bright windows of tobacco stores—I'd stop wherever there was an array—newsstands, displays of hardware, skeins of black and blonde hair hung between elaborately wigged wooden heads in beauty salons; I wanted detail to study, but a profusion so I did not have to linger long on anything. Sometimes when I got home, my mother would be on the telephone describing my coat to the police. As I prepared for bed, she'd rage outside my closed door, demanding explanations, reciting the names of children who brought their parents pleasure and honor, calling on my dear father to witness my delinquency, calling on God to witness her ordeal in having to be both a father and a mother to me. I would fall asleep in the torrent, thinking usually of the exhausted school day that awaited me. I don't know what it was that drove me downtown two or three nights a week. There were often long dark blocks between the windows I loved. Walking them, hungry for the next array, I had a heroic vision of myself: I was a man in the middle-twenties, raincoated, battered hat pulled low above intense eyes, a history of injustice in his heart, a face too noble for revenge, walking the night along some wet boulevard, followed by the sympathy of countless audiences. My creation was derived from the lonely investigations of private eyes into radio or movie crimes, family accounts of racial wandering, Bible glories of wilderness saints and hermits. My creation walked with the trace of a smile on his Captain Marvel lips, he was a master of violence, but he dealt only in peace. He knew twenty languages, all the Chinese dialects, hardly anyone had ever heard him speak. Loved by two or three beautiful women who could never have him, he was so dedicated, every child who ever saw him loved him. He wrote brilliant, difficult books and famous professors sometimes recognized him in streetcars, but he turned away and got off at the next stop. If we could ever tell it, how it happens, we grow to approximate the vision (minus the nobility, trace of smile, languages, mastery), we get what we wanted, we grow in some way towards the thirteen-year-old's dream, training ourselves with sad movies, poems of loss, minor chords of the guitar, folk songs of doomed socialist brotherhood. And soon, we are strolling the streets in a brand new trench coat, hair in careful disarray, embracing the moonlight, all the pity of the darkness in a precious kind of response to the claim of the vision, but then much later when we are tired of indulgence, and despise the attitude, we find ourselves walking the streets in earnest, in real rain, and we circle the city almost to morning until we know every wrought-iron gate, every old mansion, every mountain view. In these compulsive journeys, we become dimly aware of a new vision, we pray that it might be encouraged to grow and take possession, overwhelming the old one, a vision of order, austerity, work, and sunlight. So, it was that, last week I was moving along Pine Avenue, at four in the morning, wishing myself somewhere else, in a house of my own beside a wife, work prepared for the next day.

In my room, on Mountain Street, a beautiful girl lay asleep on a mattress and I couldn't be beside her. I was heading toward Côte-des-Neiges and she was sleeping back at my room, a profound sleep of isolation, her red hair fallen on her face and shoulders as if arranged by a Botticelli wind. I could not help thinking that she was too beautiful for me to have, that I was not tall enough or straight, that I did not command the glory of the flesh, that people did not turn to look at me in streetcars, and despite certain emotional and artistic achievements (she could also claim them), she deserved someone, an athlete perhaps, who moved with a grace equal to hers, exercised as she did, the immediate tyranny of beauty in face and limb. Two days before, the evening of the day she had come to Montreal, she told me she loved me, she said to me the words which I do not think I will ever be able to use easily, "I love you," she said them and I let them dignify us, but I did not allow them too deeply into my heart. Perhaps she knew this. I think she wanted to believe the words, but I don't think she did. Perhaps I should have forced myself to respond to her declaration. Perhaps it is best for people to establish the ideal (love) in practical terms, as quickly as possible, to bring it close, to make it a real possibility. What do I know of the words anyhow? I have fled them as though they were a sentence of bondage, I have never been able to utter them with courage. Later, on that same night, we were walking down Mountain Street to get something to eat. I showed her a lovely iron fence which had in its calligraphy silhouettes of swallows, rabbits, chipmunks. She said to me, "You've won me," and she said my name. Should I have believed that I had won her? Let men and women couple together, make the beast with two backs, cry kisses into each other's mouths, give every gift of flesh and spirit until there is no more giving or demanding but a blind divine exchange of bodies, and then let them whisper in exhausted voices, "We have won each other." Which we never managed.

By the end of the next day, I had written a stillborn poem about two armies marching to encounter from different corners of a continent. They never meet in conflict in the hungry central plain. Winter eats through the battalions like a storm of moths at a brocade gown, leaving the metal threads of artillery strewn gunner-less, miles behind the frozen men, pointless designs on a vast closet floor. Then months later, two corporals of different language meet in a green un-blasted field. Their feet are bound with strips of cloth, torn from the uniforms of superiors. This field they meet upon is the one that distant powerful marshals ordained for glory. Because the men have come from different directions, they face each other, but they have forgotten why they stumbled there. And she had done some writing too. I found the paper after she had gone.

"You cannot have me now—I pity myself too much and hate myself too much at times—you can never have me now—I want to speak but cannot now . . ."

But we went beyond this, we finally found words to say. I don't wish to record them all, even though I remember them. We spoke so that we could become tender. It was not the kind of tenderness which follows passion, but the kind which follows failure. So, I resolved to discard lust since it could not be answered. For the time remaining for us, I would regard her as the fine instrument of discipline and grace which she was and praise her trained beauty as it deserved. To be fustian: we abandoned the mattress of lovers for the close armchairs of friendship. That night, I watched her move about my room. Our conversation had emancipated her. I had never seen her so beautiful. She was nested in a brown chair, studying her script. When I worked in a foundry, I remember a color I loved in the crucible of melted brass. Her hair was that color and her warm body seemed to reflect it just as the caster's face glows above the poured molds. As she repeated the famous words to herself, her face was a child at First Communion or an old lady's in a remembered pilgrimage of virginity. I thought the exclamation of Baudelaire, *mon semblable*:

PAUVRE GRANDE BEAUTÉ!
POOR PERFECT BEAUTY!

I yielded all my silent praise for her limbs, her lips, not to the clamor of personal desire, but to the pure demand of excellence. I was detached enough to write in my notebook:

Once I longed for distance,
Miles of railroad track
To hurl my love away from me
So I could wish her back.

Now my flesh requires
What distance cannot give.
No comfort in the mental kiss;
You need my mouth to live.

I studied her marvelous body, which she had charitably left unclothed, her belly (think of the soft primitive line drawn on the cave wall by the artist-hunter and use it to outline an albino heart), and I remembered her cruel intestines:

Quel mal mystérieux ronge son flanc d'athlète?
What unknown evil harrows her lithe side?

Those were very good hours we spent together in my room. Most together because we were most apart. Poet and Actress lost in their damned Crafts. Then she was tired and lay down to sleep. She was leaving the next morning. I wanted to lie a moment by her side. I closed the lights and lay beside her. I even thought, wildly, that a miracle would deliver us into a sexual embrace, I don't know why, the natural language of bodies because we were pleasant people, because she was leaving the next morning, I don't know. We said goodnight to each other. She rested her hand on my thigh, nothing of desire in the touch. And she went to sleep, and I opened my eyes in the dark and my room was never emptier, and she was never further away. I listened to her breathing, it was like the delicate engine of some cruel machine, spreading distance after distance between us. Then I was more alone than I have ever been, and my room became intolerable. Her sleep was the final withdrawal, more perfect than anything she could say or write to me, and she slept with a deeper grace than she moved. Now I could intrude on no part of her. I kissed her hair, remembering that hair does not feel and I rose and dressed.

The night had been devised by a purist of Montreal autumns. A light rain made the black iron gates shine. Leaves lay precisely etched on the wet pavement, flat as if they had fallen from diaries. A wind blurred the small leaves of the young acacia trees on McGregor Street. And I was walking an old route of fences and

mansions I know by heart and wondering how many more
times I would have to walk it. One word rolled around in my
mind and colonized my thoughts until my only mental activity
was to repeat it again and again with each step I took. *Driven.*
Dri-ven. Dri-ven. This writing embarrasses me. I am humorist
enough to see a young man stepping out of Stendhal, given to
self-dramatization, walking off a comfortless erection. Perhaps
masturbation would have been more effective and less tiring. Let
me say only this about the walk: the rain was real, the wind and
the desperation were real, and the hat over the forehead, the
isolation of the streets, the eyes that search every shallow and
deep doorway for the soft embrace of a waiting, destined woman,
the prayer almost cried, "Help Thou my unbelief," and the cold,
beautiful rain-jeweled answer of indifference, all these were real.
The thirteen-year-old's vision was as close to materialization as
it had ever been, and for the first time, I knew that I hated it. Two
hours of walking and my head was clear, I thought of dreams,
manipulations for martyrdom, the tall exquisite women who are
sad because they cannot love, their lips I crushed my lips against,
and myself the moonlight sponge, the jukebox heart; I reviewed the
impossible predicaments I created, the impossible girls I courted,
the icy carcasses caressed, the hate returned by tenderness to
rot the heart—all these I applauded goodbye, as a cheap bur-
lesque audience applauds the last number, the puffing line of
middle-aged floozies dancing backwards into the wings with
superficial nostalgia and real revulsion. Of course, it was not a
true goodbye. I knew that there would be other nights that
I would walk through, but I would know where I preferred to be,
and I would be working toward it, and back in my room, there
would be no queenly lady sleeping alone. But that night there was.
I made a little noise coming in and she awakened.

"Oh," she said, "I wish I could have gone with you."

I did not reply. She understood that something important had happened to me and that the strain was finally over between us. I touched her face and went to bed for a few hours. We sat very close to each other during the taxi ride to the airport. It was raining still. We drove out of Montreal. When we saw the first airplanes, she breathed a little startled sigh for both of us. The car ride had been too short for the friendliness we felt.

"I'll miss you," she said, and I said that I would too.

O Mariette, no one moves as beautifully as you, no one's voice is such a perfect slave to his will, no one's hair pours so many earth and metal colors over white shoulders. The turbojet will carry to the height you deserve. Grant audience to the countryside. Your eyes are trained for continents. Half my bed is too little empire for your imperial appetite. I will always imagine you in the air, at the summit of a mountain or on the roof of a great Manhattan hotel. The punishing rain and cold air will be more welcome to your body than hands and kisses are, and you have a pure art for transmuting all your pain to silver. Burn like the cold moon men watch. Draw the camera back. Pan the airfield. Cohen is waving goodbye to one of his sharp women. He is indulging himself in a little harmless rhetoric. The plane disappears into the lead sky.

Cohen catches a limousine back to town. During the ride back, he considers the great technical achievement which an airport is. He could never organize one. Or take any new building on the way into the city. Who has the mastery to plan such a thing? In Red China, they were smelting iron in their backyards. In Israel, men and women, his own age, were fighting and farming the desert. In special schools, steel-nerved men, in perfect physical condition, were being trained to walk in areas where the gravity pull was different, they were learning to breathe alien atmospheres. Railroads, huge corporations, governments: he would never be able to grasp or work within their intricacies, and as industrial Montreal flies by the car window, he feels humble before every gas station.

Back in his room, Mariette is brought to him again. There are her sheets, there are red hairs in his brush. He finds the note written a day before. "You cannot have me now. . . ." He reads it over almost a dozen times. Then he begins this entry in his erratic journal, feeling curiously at the very center of things.

David Who?

The rain froze around eight o'clock. Cars slipping all over Mountain Street. I was walking down to the Ritz Carlton for my cousin's concert. I saw an old lady on her knees in front of a driveway.

"Why haven't they salted the road?" she screamed. "No, you can't help me."

The truth is, I don't like touching old ladies.

"I think I can help you, Madam."

I reached her my hand and I fell beside her.

"No one can help me," she said triumphantly.

The only old lady I ever liked was Queen Mary. I crawled over to a path of frozen mud. I managed to stand, and I pulled her over. It was only a few doors down to her apartment.

"You're a very nice young man. This is the second time I've ever fallen in my life."

I knew she was lying, but I didn't care to question her. She was staring at me. "Now I'm going to do *you* a favor. Tidy yourself up. Your clothes. Your hair. You'll do a lot better in this world. Goodnight."

"Thank you, Madam."

My cousin's concert was a flop. She sat down in front of the piano, and after a long silence, it was apparent that she'd forgotten how the piece began. She went out and came back with the music and a look of real terror. She mangled everything she played. Her fingers were made of rubber bands. But a pretty girl. I spoke to her father in the Intermission.

"Very fine, once she got going."

"Terrible, you mean," he said cheerfully. "Comes by it naturally. Couldn't speak in public 'til I was forty. Sweat so much my shoes sloshed when I left the stage. She's only fifteen, lots of time."

"Fifteen. I didn't think she was that old."

"You could use a haircut, boy."

"Yes, sir."

The second part of the program was an entertainment by a Korean deaf-mute of about thirty who played the xylophone. He held the mallets like weapons and looked at us all with hatred. I wished he would leap into the audience and crack heads, but he finished his rendition of a Korean folk song. Nor did the hate leave his eyes while his trainer made a speech telling of his plans to teach all the deaf-mutes of the East to play the xylophone and bring them into the wonderful world of music. At the Reception for the Artists, I caught the deaf-mute when he was out of his trainer's sight. I slipped a joint of marijuana into his jacket pocket.

"Smokey, smokey," I whispered, tapping my lips with two fingers.

My cousin was rather happy to be out noticed by the deaf-mute. She was very nearly hiding behind a curtain.

"Very fine, once you got going."

She was too embarrassed to talk.

"Very fine, indeed."

She tried to say something.

"Liked it, liked it very much," I pressed on.

"Damn you," she blurted. "Damn you, damn my father, and how dare you come to my recital with your horrible bohemian hair?"

The next morning, I phoned her. I lay the receiver on the bed and played her some Bach on my guitar.

"That's how it's supposed to sound," I said.

"God, I hate you."

"I'll call tomorrow the same time. I have a lot to teach you."

"Don't."

I planned a day of meditation and prayer. I had a very good bath in the afternoon. I loved my bathroom. I read last Saturday's newspaper. I was happy all that misery was safely in the past. Old earthquakes and withered crimes disturbed me not at all. One thing is sure: I know how to relax in a bathtub. It was the telephone that got me out. Gloria Rosez. She said that she had saved enough money to buy a bottle of cognac. Would I like to kill it with her?

"You got me out of the bath, Gloria."

"I'm sorry."

"And I never go back to a bath I've got out of."

"I said I was sorry."

"All right, Gloria. Goodbye."

"What about the Hennessy?" she asked weakly.

"I have dedicated this day."

I had a wonderful hour or two making my bed. I paid a lot of money for that bed. One of these days, I'm going to buy another pillow. Right now, I have two pillows, and neither is made out of foam rubber, thank you very much. I paid special attention to the bedspread. A bedspread should cover the blankets and sheets, the way clothes should cover a beautiful woman, giving the true forms, distorting nothing, yet yielding surprise and delight when peeled away. I put on my duffle coat and opened the only window in the room. There was a clock on my windowsill. I noticed that I looked out of the window from 4:35 to 6:15. I could see nothing unusual or untoward. My pleasure was intense. Soon my room became very cold. All the human smells were killed. I closed the window and broke wind a few times to restore the homey quality of the atmosphere. Then I tended to my marijuana plants. Actually, they were just shoots. I watered them, I gave them a long sunlamp treatment, I said the usual prayers. From last year's harvest, I rolled up a large joint. Close to midnight, the telephone rang.

"It's Gloria. My mother has committed suicide."

"That's very inventive, Gloria. But you can't come over."

"Listen to me."

"I am listening. I have broken up my life to listen."

"Well, couldn't it have happened? Things like that happen. That's what nobody understands. Things like that happen every day."

"That's true. Come now. Hurry."

Her hair was down in my honor. I read her my favourite parts of the Saturday paper and we laughed a good deal. I will say that Gloria smokes too much. I do not like to have to worry about rolling on an ashtray. She discovered a butt sticking to her thigh.

Just before she left, she said, "You look like David, standing there."

"David who?"

"King David. Your hair."

I kissed her, a hundred and fifty times, my teacher of that night. Fools, fools across the whole city, what do any of you know about hair, why do you consent to so much pain? It was almost morning now, so I phoned my cousin.

"You'd better come down here right away."

"I will not!"

"I think I'm sick. I can't move the whole left side of my body."

"Are you serious?"

"I'm scared."

"Be right over."

I straightened the bed, emptied the ashtrays, hid my little marijuana orchard. I had a plan for the day. After my cousin would leave, no matter what happened, I'd send a Valentine's card, a lacey big one, to the old lady who had torn her stockings and made her knees bloody on the ice.

Short Story on Greek Island

This happened on one of the Greek islands. It doesn't matter which one because they are all becoming pretty much alike—in the same way and for the same reasons that cities became alike. Angus Stern settled back in the canvas chair and crossed his bare feet on the wicker one. The wasps attacked his baclava. When one grounded itself in the honey, he merely carved around it. He hadn't yet acquired the courage to catch them in midair and crush them in his fist, the way the waiters did. He was sure that skill would come.

The tourists squeezed out of the port side of the Nereida. Proprietors of empty beds greeted them with smiles and prices quoted in American currency. Donkey men stood silently, apparently considering their beasts advertisement enough. An embarrassed middle-aged woman fought with a six-year-old child who, unbidden, had managed to get his shoulder under a rather large valise. She had to give him silver to get it back and satisfy her notions about child labor. The bright crowd bobbed down the quay. This was Angus Stern's parade and the highlight of his morning—*his* morning which did not quite correspond to the mornings of less fortunate people. It was two o'clock in the afternoon and the baclava was his breakfast. He

was watching for a girl with unbound hair who didn't carry
a camera or a plastic bag and who probably wore slacks and san-
dals. There was bound to be one in this load because there
hadn't been one for several days. A group of young Athenians
passed him, their heads bandaged under straw hats in last year's
Riviera style and their radios tuned to three different stations.
Yorgo charged into the procession and tried to snare a party of
watercolorists by waving a red crayfish in their faces and shouting the word *wonderful* in three languages. It didn't look too
promising. Angus Stern was a connoisseur of the type he awaited.
He had trained in the coffee shops of New York, Montreal, and
London. They were usually surprised when they learned he was
a businessman and he used the surprise to his advantage. All the
other men were small and kind of caved in and working on
a masterpiece. The Greek island was a glorious extension of the
Carmen, the Figaro, and the Troubadour.

And the girls that came this far were definitely committed
to adventure. The crowd, deserted by those who decided to eat,
shop, or sightsee, moved toward the concrete bathing platforms.
The slaughterhouse formerly stood here but it had been removed
to a less valuable location. Very early in the morning, out of habit,
many of the natives still dumped their garbage from this point.
Oh well, he could always struggle with the Athenian shop girls.
Maybe they knew French. The Beat Generation had failed him
for over a week. Maybe he'd hit Rhodes. He'd heard there was
quite a colony down there. He clapped his hands louder than
necessary. A woman sat down close by who was dressed just the
way he hated. He hated her way more than the plastic shoes and
iridescent blouses of the economy class. He associated it with
something unwholesome like soiled elaborate lingerie. She was
wearing a rather old-fashioned white dress with lace trimming

on the collar, sleeves, and hem. An area of the hem had been burned by careless ironing. Women who think that frills make them feminine. A second glance informed him that she wasn't a woman but a girl very pale and even beautiful if you like T.B. heroines. But there were wrinkles on her neck which showed even though she held her head high to stretch them out. How old was she, anyway?

"I guess you live here," she said.

"What?"

"You're staring at me, so I asked you if you live here."

"Yes. Yes, I live here."

"I guess you're a painter or writer or anthropologist, or what?"

Her voice was charming. The innocence was practised but well practised. He recovered quickly.

"Actually, I do nothing. I'm retired."

She laughed, and her teeth could have been whiter.

"I passed a very strenuous adolescence," he explained his old joke. "What do you do?"

"I'm a kind of whore."

He was almost caught off-guard a second time. It was a long while since he'd been shoved around in an opening.

"What kind?"

"The kind people would never call one."

"Oh, just a woman."

He believed he was back in form. His pastry dish was studded with drowned and struggling wasps. One detached itself and gained the air. He snatched at it, gave it too much room in his fist and cried in pain. The woman stood up and by the way her dress remained creased, even in his discomfort, he could swear she wasn't wearing underwear. She wanted to help.

"I've got something in my house. Want to see my house?"

"I hope you don't have to go through this ordeal every time you want to take someone home."

"Shut up, shut up," he felt like telling her, as they began the whitewashed steps. He hoped the lady who ran the little grocery wouldn't rush out with a gardenia, as she did every time he passed her store with a woman. They couldn't find the stinger. She dragged him by the finger to the window, so she could have a good look. He kissed her hair. She threw his hand down violently.

"Don't touch me! I'm pregnant."

She relaxed immediately and sat down in the carved Samos chair.

"Can I stay here tonight? My name is Martha."

"Lots of room," he demonstrated with his swelling hand. The pathetic part of her appealed to him.

———

Like many young Americans, Angus Stern saw his revolution in terms of idleness and an infinite number of female bodies. He managed the first part by having very cautious parents who habitually took out flight insurance from those machines in the lobbies of airports. As for the second, he worked on the theory that imaginative people were promiscuous. His new money enabled him to graduate from espresso bars to Art Colonies and everywhere that wasn't the U.S. was an Art Colony. It seemed to him that all the young Americans in Europe were artists or intellectuals or oddballs. He was the only straight man left. He still described himself as a businessman, although he had no plans for the next two years, at least, and when a young German, who spoke English with a hillbilly accent, asked him if he was a writer he said, "No, thank you, I'm a reader." Sometimes he felt America was speeding somewhere without him. This was usually when flesh was too plentiful or too scarce. He had a good memory and comforted himself with visualizations of the rat race. American opportunity looked better from the outside. He wouldn't have missed this for anything. The kook of a girl was taking off that dress right in front of him.

"I'm hot. Can I lie down? Isn't everybody supposed to go to sleep this time of day?"

"That's a bed." He took her hand to lead her there.

"Don't be silly," she said. "When a girl is pregnant, she has to be treated like a sister."

"You don't look pregnant," he justified himself.

"Well, stop looking."

One for the books, he congratulated himself as she began faintly snoring. She didn't look pregnant at all. She was thin, but her skin hung loosely on the long bones of her limbs like a flag whipped by the wind around the pole. And there were funny marks on her shoulders and buttocks. Suddenly, all the desire she provoked changed to pity. What kind of life did she have, anyway, drifting from one bed to another, guarding her pride by a bold show, hoping for shelter here and there. Not him. He wasn't going to take advantage. He covered her with a fresh sheet and himself with the cool antiseptic of a resolution. He would salvage her. His life wasn't such a mess, he wasn't such a bastard. Purpose wasn't confined to America. She wasn't very pretty when you saw her naked. He changed his mind when he gave her a shower on the terrace. Goose pimples tightened up her skin and breasts. Her hair became dark and clung to her high-boned face like the hood of a Madonna. He found himself wielding the bucket with unnecessary vehemence.

"Be careful," she cried. "I don't want to slip. Oh, listen!"

She took his hand and held it flat against her wet stomach. He couldn't feel anything. A wave of anger against her openness swept through him. Sister, my ass. I'm only human if she goes on this way. But he had made a resolution and he was anxious to prove that hot countries didn't eat a strong man's will.

———

"Blokes have made my wife before, but I don't like The Enemy up her pants. You're The Enemy, Master Angus. I'd forgotten about them, but they sent one right into my parlour all dressed up as a human. Being."

This was quietly spoken by the Australian writer, Sidney Gearston, as he opened the door of the courtyard for Angus Stern two nights before.

"But you said it happened before, Sid, so you can't really hold . . ."

"Get out, Stern."

Oh, well, they drink too much anyway, he consoled himself on the way home. He was frankly surprised that Gearston would take it so hard. After all, look at the stuff in his books. Nevertheless, in that part of the mind, where guilt extends hospitality to insult, the stinging final three syllables remained. That was the first time he'd be thrown out of a man's house and even if the man happened to be a dipso. The episode was fresh enough to influence his answer when Martha asked him for a loan.

"Two hundred dollars? Is that all it costs?"

"It was even less in Havana. But that's all over now."

"How many have you had?" he said casually.

"Apparently, an insufficient number. I'm still hopelessly fertile."

"C'mon, it's not so smart to talk like that."

He hated her for a second, even if she was joking. Sometimes these people could profit by horsewhipping, it seemed to him.

"Hey!" He tried to look inspired as he commenced his work of salvage. "I got an idea: why don't you *have* it?"

He couldn't quite interpret the smile she gave him, but he wanted to wipe it off her face with his fist. It said something like: "I only deal with men." The smile dismissed him with an arrogant invitation he couldn't answer.

"Can you manage it or not?"

He considered kicking her out then and there.

"I'll sign some traveller's cheques. You can cash them on the port tomorrow." He looked at his watch. "The bank closes in five minutes."

"Do it now, Angus, please. I can make it."

He blotted his signature and handed the cheques to her solemnly.

"I'd like to talk to you, Martha."

"We have all night," she laughed on the run.

His hand was beginning to hurt. Sure, you could call him a sucker, but he knew these people and you had to get their confidence first. She was very graceful when she ran, and she had left her hair free because it was still damp. He was sure he could straighten her out.

The mountain turned orange, then glowing amber, then dead rust, looking toward the port like a slow tidal wave as it changed color. In the midst of the last change, it was suddenly night. They were eating together at Yorgo's and he wished she wouldn't drink so much. He gulped down a large glass of retsina and emptied the rest of the flask into his glass to save her from it. He was going to tell her why she should go back home and tell her family and have the kid. Her dress appeared snowy and fresh in the light shed by a stand of weak electric bulbs. A yacht sneaked into the harbour and a hundred Greek teenagers screamed toward it with autograph books to ruin Elizabeth Taylor's vacation. Yorgo explained that the returning fishermen had spread the word she was coming hours ago.

"I don't know why I should, but I believe in you," said Angus Stern.

"Of course, you do—I'm very believable in. Can I have some of yours?"

Then Yorgo was bending over the table with a full flask. For a fraction of a second, their hands wrestled over the glass.

"I didn't order that."

"I offer *pedimu*, I offer. To celebrate the American sputnik that comes over us tonight."

He looked twenty-five, but Angus knew he was forty. Angus Stern didn't want to hear about the American sputnik. Martha stood up and kissed Yorgo on both cheeks. A thin handsome man passing the table recognized her.

"Martha Prochert! I knew you'd find this delicious island eventually!"

"Lorrie, Lorrie, sit *down!*"

But before he sat down, this man, whom Angus considered the biggest pervert he'd ever met, was kissed by Martha. Lawrence Monderhan was supposed to be a painter, but he was on the island, not for the light or pretty scenes, but for the Naval School. Yorgo presented Lorrie with a full glass and a plate of olives and Angus Stern knew his evening was finished.

"You with *him?*" Lorrie asked with fake incredulity.

"Anything the matter with that?" Angus Stern said, with genuine belligerence.

"Angus is very sweet," she answered the first question.

"He is, I *know* he is," he said, with what Angus thought was a tone of lying familiarity. "But is he your *type?*"

"He will be. Oh, Lorrie, I haven't seen you since New York and that was hell."

"Well, darling, *this* is Paradise and I'm never going to leave. Even the *police* love me here, don't they, Yorgo?"

Yorgo fingered the buckle of his wide belt.

"That's supposed to excite me," Lorrie explained.

Not only was his evening of salvage completely destroyed, but Angus Stern knew he was going to end up paying for the wine. Lawrence Monderhan was just the type of person she shouldn't have anything to do with. He had fascinated Angus for a week or two and Angus had bought him a lot of dinners. Then, as a sort of reciprocating, Lorrie had invited him to a little session up the hill beside the cannon. Angus Stern was allowed to watch the young sailors beat Lawrence Monderhan until he could no longer embrace them. "They love us, they absolutely *love* us," Lorrie roared to the port in general, and then confidentially to Martha, "You know, it's the first time I've ever been popular at school."

"Naval School," Angus Stern supplied, unnecessarily and bitterly.

Lorrie grabbed Angus Stern's wrist and twisted it toward him so that he could read the time—a habit that annoyed Angus Stern from the beginning, but most especially because of the wasp sting.

"Lord! It'll be in the sky any minute now. Let's get up to the Gearston's. Sidney will *like* you, Martha, won't he, Angus?"

"Are they having another party?"

"Another party, are you *mad*? Sidney's been talking about nothing else for *days*. Haven't you heard him go on about 'a new light to enflame the old constellations'? Everybody, you know, the old *everybody*, will be there. Sidney's calling it The-Down-With-Spengler-Revival-Of-The-West-Satellite-Gazing-Party!"

"Any excuse to get drunk."

"C'mon, Angus," said Martha, "it sounds like fun."

"You go for the experience. I can't take another Gearston mob."

"That's right, Martha, you come for the experience. You really ought to get *around* more, you poor sheltered thing."

Before she got up, she leaned forward and said softly, "But I'll see you later tonight, won't I, Angus, at home?"

Her face was beautiful, no question about it, a thin child's face that he wanted to kiss, that he didn't want Lorrie to take away. She was definitely worthwhile.

"Sure."

He watched it sail across the sky, a new star with a fiery tail, impudent and innocent and majestic, and he held his breath, so it wouldn't fall. It made its way through the ancient zodiac like a very young pilgrim, high above the calm yachts, the small songs of the port, the floating islands of the Aegean Sea and it caused Angus Stern to be proud and nostalgic. Yorgo watched it with him, and Savaz, who used to be carpenter, but was now a real estate agent selling white houses to foreigners. Angus Stern wished he could have seen it with people who spoke English.

Back at his house he studied drawings of the satellite in the Herald Tribune, to pass the time until she came back. Where was she, anyway? The Gearston's parties never lasted that long. Two hours later, he was furious and wanted to wash his hands of all of them, the Gearstons, the Lorries, the Marthas, all the driftwood.

Worse than driftwood: scum. It was insane to get mixed up with these people. He walked aimlessly down to the sea. The stars were still bright and huge, but the night had faded from its deep royal blue. An orange peel that someone had removed very carefully bobbed beside the bathing platform like a waterlily. He began to climb to the fortress because he needed perspective. He wanted a clear view. A hundred and forty years ago, brave men had won their freedom. He wanted to stand in the atmosphere of discipline and courage.

But don
　　step on my bloo svede shoos...

He ran toward the voices, knowing what he would find but unable to restrain himself. The young Greeks were shouting the song drunkenly and beating their belts against the rocks in time. Lorrie was naked, performing a bizarre dance with Martha. The sailors cheered as he pulled her brutally from their midst. There was no end to the entertainment the strangers could provide. He had a hold of her arm; he'd never let it go; he stumbled down the hill with her, telling her he loved her. They faced each other on the concrete platform, both gasping.

"You ruined a perfectly lovely evening," Martha said, "but you'll pay for it. It's about time you started paying."

"What are you talking about? I pay for everything! I paid for dinner, I'm paying for your goddam abortion, you people are the greatest spongers I..."

She extracted a roll of Greek bills from a lace pocket and held it to her lips.

"You really didn't believe I was pregnant, did you?"

"Gimme that!"

He lashed out for the money, she tilted her face, his hand struck her jaw.

"Oh, I'm sorry!"

She didn't wince, she smiled as she had in the afternoon. He didn't want to understand it, but he did.

"You're the same as . . ."

"And you!"

His heart pounded like waves in a cavern. The black was returning to the sky where the new star was lost like a kite he had let go. But doors were opening in the black and he'd always wanted to pass through them, all his life. But he was twenty-eight, and in twelve years he'd be forty. But vast doors were opening on to the deepest black ever as she stretched herself out on the platform like a patient.

"That's it, that's it, that's nice," she whispered in pain, as he aimed his swollen fist again and again.

ive had lots of pets

daddy is awful important in the museum and they often send him
to far away places to bring back things and plants so everybody
can study them   mommy doesnt like it when daddy goes away
and she says o be careful o be careful but daddy says there there
now there there now until mommy stops crying and he goes
anyways   i dont mind when daddy goes because he is awful
important in the museum and so they take good care of him
because they dont want anything to happen to him   besides
he always brings me back something to play with   one time he
brought me a funny plant that had a hard hard stem and when
i put it in the sun after a while it grew little red balls that daddy
said i could eat and i did but i ate too many and got sick   one time
he brought me a bird that sang very pretty and mommy would
play nice music and the pretty bird would sing but once i killed it
by mistake   daddy did not mind too much and said that he
would bring me another pet to play with next time the museum
sends him away   soon mommy got sad again so i knew that
daddy was going away again   goodbye goodbye he said to everyone dont worry and you take good care of your mother he said to
me   mommy stood very close to me and said o be careful and
please please write to me and daddy said o yes of course now dont

you worry again   after daddy left mommy showed me a picture
of daddy and his friends in the newspaper and a big story about
how important he was and a new place that he was supposed to
be going to   daddy was gone a long time but we knew he was
all right because of the letters he sent   mommy told me that he
had found the new place and was coming back soon with all sorts
of things for the museum and also a pet for me goody goody   soon
daddy came back and we went to meet him   everyone was there
guards and policemen and very important people and they all
cheered when daddy came out and shook his hands   we are
all proud of you a great service to your country and history making or something they said that night mommy and daddy went
out together but before they left daddy told me he had brought
a pet back for me but i could not have it until the museum was
finished   o thank you i said   and i could hardly wait   one night
daddy came home from work and he had a box with him   come
here and see what ive got here he said   he put the box on the
floor and opened it up   mommy could not look but i don't blame
her because they were awful ugly smelly pets daddy had brought
home   o take them away she said daddy i said why did you
bring 2   one is a boy pet and one is a girl pet daddy said   o
i said   gosh i never saw anything so funny looking and hairy such
a funny shape with 5 points   but mommy was crying and daddy
said all right all right we wont keep them and he said to me look
these pets arent too smart so they wont make very good pets but
i said i want them i want them i want them and i started crying
too   and there was lots of noise with me crying and mommy
crying and daddy shouting but I got my way   daddy finally got
quiet and said i should feed them because they hadnt eaten for
a long time had to clean on the cage so often and it was part of
an experiment   in the box they were like tied up together but

when i put in the piece of food they both rushed for it and made
funny noises and started fighting for the food ha ha ha ha i said
and so did daddy but mommy wouldnt look   after that i took
care of them all by myself   three times they tried to get away but
i found them and put them in a bigger box   once when i was
putting some food in the box they tried to stick something into
my tentacle so i stung them dead   never mind said daddy we
have lots more in the museum and kissed the sore spot with his
other mouth—HERE IS A WHOLE PLANET FULL OF THEM

Strange Boy with a Hammer

Josh put his knife and fork carefully beside his plate.

"Mama," he asked, "Mama, do you like the spring? I mean, do you like it?"

Mrs. Eliezer felt the warm eyes on her and leaned forward to clasp her son's hand.

"Yes, *liebele*, I like the spring. I like it very much."

"I do too, Mama, but it is sad."

"Sad?"

"Yes, because last year's leaves are dead, and no one remembers them. Everyone is so happy with the new buds that last year's leaves are forgotten."

"That is true, Josh, but you remember them. Maybe that is enough."

"Yes, Mama, I suppose that is enough. Yes, it is enough."

"Now try to eat your supper."

Before he left the table, he asked, "May I take some vinegar to my room, Mama?"

"Vinegar? But what for, my son?"

"I would like some in my room. May I, Mama?"

"Take it in one of the little glasses, then. Be careful not to spill the bottle."

A strange child, my child, she thought, as she heard him mount the stairs. Thirteen and so small, he hardly eats. And so quiet. And always by himself, always by himself. And every night now, working on the wood. It had started three weeks ago when he had brought the large pieces into the house.

"What will you do with this wood, Josh?" she'd asked.

"I am taking it to my room. May I, Mama?"

"Of course, but what is it for, *mine liebele?*"

"Oh, I will shave and polish it until it shines like glass. Then I'll stain it with . . ."

"All right, *liebele,*" she had replied.

And now spring, leaves and vinegar. It is a hard, hard thing, not to know your son, not to understand your son. It is not right that a boy should grow up so alone. Ach, if only his father were still here. He would know what to do. And such a brave boy, with his Bar Mitzvah next week, and not even nervous. Yesterday she had spoken to him.

"Mrs. Katz tells me her Israel is so nervous about his Bar Mitzvah that he hardly sleeps. Are you afraid too, my *kasavitza?*"

"Sometimes, Mama, but mostly no. I know my Portion and besides, it is a long way off."

"But it is next Sabbath."

"Well, that is a long time, Mama. You always say, 'we never know what tomorrow brings.'"

"Ah, your father would have been so proud to see you in the Synagogue, reciting the Torah. We are all so proud of you."

"Thank you, Mama," he had said.

With a sigh Mrs. Eliezer rose from the table and started to clear the dishes. "Ach, I will do them tomorrow. I need some air," she said, almost aloud. In the backyard the smells of young green life mingled with her thoughts. A tired moon hung above the nascent trees and she fixed her eye on it, only vaguely aware of the beauty about her.

"What the moon knows," she said in Yiddish, remembering what her mother used to say, "what the moon knows, only little children know. Only little children know the stars and what the clouds are made of. Only little children can watch a candle and say, it sings a song. Only little children can see birds and cry, 'look, all the pigeons have red feet.' And only little children can weep for last year's leaves and find spring sad. Only little children. Only little children."

Mrs Eliezer sank into a garden chair and covered her face with her hands. She felt old and very tired. Rocking back and forth she hummed, "*Oif'n Pripichick, brent a firerle . . .*"

Distant city bells chimed nine o'clock. *Bang, ba-bang, bang,* came the sound of hammering from the house.

"What is my strange little boy doing with his hammer now, what is my strange little boy doing with his hammer now?" she hummed to the same tune. Soon she was asleep.

She shivered. She didn't know how she had slept that long. Four o'clock. She paused in front of Josh's door, before deciding to enter the room. The door seemed to stick as she pushed it open. She walked to his bed and in a flash of horror realized he wasn't in it. Frantically, she sought the bed lamp. Then she saw Josh. He was hanging by one hand from a large cross of polished wood which was fastened to the door. In his other hand, he held a hammer. He had bled to death.

Trade

Stealing down the stairs, he didn't hate his father, creeping down the front hall at three in the morning, Tony Francis didn't hate his father, sending out his hand like a hunting falcon into the folds of the clothes closet, he resented not his father, nor mother, nor childhood, nor schooling, not even his own mistakes. The hand registered the expensive softness of his father's cashmere sport jacket, it plunged into one pocket, explored confined emptiness, retreated, clawed for the pocket on the other side, dove and extracted the car keys. He could leave his father alone as long as his father left him alone. Even if his father tried to bug him, Dr. Stryker, in his silent way, had taught Tony a sweet indifference, had taught him, during the months in the hospital and the hours later in the office, that it really didn't matter what his father thought of him, didn't matter, he had his life before him. And that was a good long time from the time the gardener had found him drunk and struggling in the front seat of the Olds, the garage door closed and the motor running, and had bullied Tony into the living room saying, "Can't understand it, sir, fellow of sixteen with all the world to hope for." His father hadn't wanted to send Tony to a hospital, but his mother had cried, threatened to leave herself and really disgrace him if that was what he was so worried about. Didn't he know his son was sick? She hurled her hatred at him when he agreed to send Tony to a hospital, but it had to be a hospital out of town. Was he ashamed of his own son? He was, damn her, he was. But when she had started to pack, he had given in.

"All right, all right, take him to any damn place you want to."

She took him to Dr. Stryker, who was well known, and Stryker had him placed in the Allan Memorial Institute of Psychiatry, which was hard to get into because of a long waiting list and a reputation for being one of the best places of its kind in the world. The Institute was housed in a converted mansion, a wartime gift of Lord and Lady Allan, style of Italian Renaissance, built on the south slope of Mount Royal. They started to work on Tony with drugs and talk and electricity. They changed him a little, made him a little happier, taught him not to care so much. He made a lot of friends, which was part of the treatment, wives who were losing their husbands to waitresses, mothers whose sons had betrayed them, boys and girls his own age who didn't quite understand what was wanted from them. At one of the Recreational Therapy dances, he met Nancy Spector.

"Are you a visitor?" she asked.

And Tony confessed, no, he was a patient.

She was nineteen and had started to whisper in his ear with her tongue a few seconds after they had started to dance. A nurse, whom everyone called Melzie, had come over and taken her arm and asked her gently if maybe she wasn't a little too tired for dancing, and walked with her into the hospital. This was during the spring when the dances were held outside on the stone floor of what must have been Lady Allan's conservatory. He had fallen in love with Nancy immediately, the sound of her tongue in his ear rattling in his groin, promising to fulfill all his fantasies. After

Nancy had been taken away, he sat on the grass and looked at the lights of the city below and wondered when he would be able to get out of this place. Then he wandered behind the buildings, up the slope of the old mountain, and stood under the lilac trees which were in full bloom. Melzie missed him back at the dance and came after him. He watched her coming toward him with satisfaction, watching her white shoes paddle through the dark grass, wanting her to speak to him. She did speak to him as they walked down the slope to the stone floor and she danced with him five times.

His father had hardly spoken to him since he had got back from the hospital, but he had learned not to let that worry him too much. Besides, now he had something very important to think about and that was Nancy Spector whom he had met that afternoon at the Allan. He hadn't seen her since the dance and when he bumped into her in front of Lord Allan's bust in the lobby, he felt the same deep rattle. They were both on their way to their doctors. She was already late for her appointment and she had to hurry, but she said she would love to see him and talk about the Old Ruin, which is what she called the Institute. Tonight was no good and tomorrow night was no good, wait a second, could he meet her late that night or didn't he think he'd be able to get out?

"I can make it, all right," he told her in his deepest voice and they agreed on a corner to meet at.

Then he went in to see Stryker, but he didn't tell him about meeting Nancy Spector.

He held the car key in his hand and swung the leather holder as though it were a small broken necked bird. He descended the steps to the basement and went into the garage which smelled of oil and leaves. He slid into the Olds, the leather seat cooled right through his trousers. Everything clicked beautifully, he felt like a master technician. Switching the ignition sounded like an expensive camera shutter. The sound of the motor grew in the garage. He worked the transmitting device which raised the garage doors automatically, shot the car into the dark yard. So, what if his father found out? It was nothing compared to some of the things he had done, like stealing money from the school office or being caught in the bathroom with his cousin. Besides, he was only taking the crate for a few hours, besides, the old man had been fairly careful with him since he'd come back from the hospital. Nancy Spector was at the corner. She was wearing a striped Italian sweater and black slacks. She opened the door herself although Tony was going to get out and open it for her. He felt suddenly shy as she nestled beside him.

"It's great to be rich, not powerful, just simply rich. I'm not wearing a bra, I can't stand a bra in the summer," she said, all in one breath.

Tony mumbled that it didn't matter, he didn't know what he was supposed to say to that. As they drove downtown, she said she'd liked him the first time she'd seen him because he looked like Keats, only he was probably bigger than Keats and she hoped he was much healthier than Keats. Had he ever seen a picture of Keats? He answered that he hadn't and hoped she wouldn't ask any more questions because although he had heard the name, he wasn't sure what Keats had done in history and besides they hadn't taken him in school. Then she asked him if he had told his doctor that he was meeting her that night and he said no, defiantly, as though he were denying a charge of tattletale. Well, she had told hers and he had said, "Nancy," he wasn't going to tell her *what* to do, or not to do, he was only there to help her understand *why* she would do, or not do, so she could make her own decisions in a more enlightened way.

"Let's take a look at the poor, dear, queer folk," said Nancy, and she told him to drive to the St. Moritz at the corner of Stanley and Ste. Catherine.

He parked the car and when he stepped out on the bright corner, he felt very much less confident without the Olds around him. She said, once more, that she wasn't wearing a bra, not that anyone *here* would care. It was a big chrome place, not another woman there. There were men sitting at the fountain or in close conspiratorial groups around arborite tables. They seemed to use a lot of hair tonic, sides of their heads looked shiny and wet. Most of them seemed thin, they were wearing tight chinos with belts in the back and many had on V-necked sweaters without shirts. Several men waved to Nancy and she waved back in a friendly manner. She whispered to Tony that they were fairly low-class pansies and no Ivy League pansy would be found dead here, but they were wonderful anyhow, they were her people, beautiful, tender, bitchy, and marvelously sick. As she talked in this extravagant vein, Tony was wondering about his hands. He sent them curled into pocket nests, leaning back at the same time, to make the gesture masculine. He let his hands confine the ache in his groin. He wished he were older and knew some place to take her. No, he no longer loved her. She was, what his mother would call, common. Still, if he were any sort of man at all, they could have a night of it. Where could he take her, would they believe him at a motel, did he have enough money? Nancy was almost as tall as he was. She wore her hair long. Tony thought that she didn't have quite the right kind of hair to wear long, it was a little on the frizzy side. She was thin, her fingers lean, the ring on one she had made snug by wrapping adhesive tape around it. Her eyes were black, small, always trying to get his eyes fastened to them as if his eyes were holes and hers were hooks, but he didn't feel like looking too hard at her. She aimed them over the coffee cup and said that she would be the sinful older woman in his life. She hoped he wouldn't disappoint her by telling her that he hadn't saved his sixteen-year-old virtue for her, sixteen years was such a long time. When she saw him drop his eyes painfully at the number sixteen, she said very gently that it was hard for her to be gentle. She touched his cheek.

"Don't listen to me, Tony, I'm just a bitch."

This gesture gave him courage. He understood it as meaning that she was stepping down a little, giving up part of her command to be more of a girl. He decided to tell her his important story, the one with the trouble in it, how he always felt that he wasn't the son his father wanted, how that feeling made him do really stupid things. For instance, last winter when he was making a real effort to please his father, he had come home one night and called Tony aside with a wink, and slipped him a package of Sheiks and told him he was pretty much a man now, and gave him the address of a place where he had made an appointment for him, and told him the name of the girl to ask for and what to do. He had gone through with it on the set day and hated it because it was so cold. After that, things had got really bad and he ended up in the garage with the motor going, struggling with the gardener, not really wanting to kill himself, but wanting to punish everyone. He told all this to Nancy, trying not to sound too young, trying to present it like a *problem* that was how he had been taught to look at it. He hoped that this disclosure would put them on more even ground because, after all, they had met at a place where problems were examined.

He was disappointed at the bitterness in her voice when she said, "You're in the club, Tony, you're in the club."

But he didn't let it bother him too much because he told himself, well, what could he expect from her, he knew what *her* problem was. When they left the St. Moritz, the same men waved after her. They got back into the comfortable car. He didn't try to open the door for her this time. She suggested they go for a little drive. He hoped it wouldn't be too long, he didn't want to lose out and he was worried because she didn't snuggle close to him like she did the first time. Maybe he shouldn't have told her anything, it seemed to have cooled her, but didn't she invite it when she touched his cheek? Melzie wouldn't have reacted like that. They drove through the heart streets of Montreal. Nancy leaned her head against the window glass, very intent on the dark city around her. The streets were changing, the Victorian gingerbread going down everywhere. On every second corner, there was the half covered skeleton of a new flat office building. The city seemed fierce to go modern as though it had been converted suddenly to some new theory of hygiene, which excluded the time dirtied Victorian stones. Nancy said that in ten years Sherbrooke Street would look like Fifth Avenue. Then she suggested that they take a look at the Old Ruin, their *Alma Mater*, at least they weren't going to pull *that* down.

He shot the car up Peel Street, proud of the way it climbed, and he parked on Pine Avenue. Above Pine, rose the southern slope of Mount Royal. There were wooden steps you could take right up the side of the mountain to the lookout. They got out of the car, crossed the street and began to climb the road through the trees that led to the wooden steps. To their left was the Institute and when they got even with it, they sat down and laughed. The towers of the Italian building looked sinister and exciting. Nancy said that they were medieval travellers at the edge of a forest and there was the castle of the cruel dwarf. Then they stared at it silently. Tony thought to himself that it was too big for jokes. And he wasn't interested in jokes, he was looking for an opening. Nancy stroked her hair and pulled some white matter from just above her forehead.

"They always make a mess of my hair," she said.

Tony knew she meant the paste they used to fasten the electrodes to her scalp for the shocks. He got them too.

"You can't notice it," he said.

He thought this was the right time, so he held his breath and tried to kiss her because it was getting late, it would soon be light. She said he was very clumsy, but very sweet and she would make everything very easy for him. She released his hands to flutter over her small breasts and he had his pleasure even before he touched her stomach. He didn't know what to do. She didn't seem to mind, merely gathered her striped sweater back into her slacks, and started talking. He wasn't listening. He was angry with himself for not getting the real thing. Down there was the city growing taller and richer every week. Nancy started to talk wildly. She said it was all a joke, a beautiful joke. The heart of the city wasn't down there among the new buildings and widening streets, the heart of the city was right over there at the Allan which, with drugs and electricity, was keeping the business men sane and their wives from suicide and their children free from hatred, that the hospital was the true heart of the city, pumping stability and erections and orgasms and sleep, into all the withering commercial limbs. Tony was not following her, he was too deep in his anger. He had been cheated. Suddenly she turned on him.

"You're not listening, not that it matters."

She said that because it was a beautiful night or morning, she should say, and because he looked like Keats, she was going to do something for him he might remember. Maybe it would be the first time, for this at least. She leaned into his lap and gave him an expert gift of mouth and tongue. He was delighted and appalled, not only with the pleasure but with the acquiring of a new dimension of experience, something he could keep. Soon he drove her back to the corner. He was very isolated from her because of his new treasure, he was turning it over in his mind, wondering what he could do with it. She leaned against the window, accustomed to isolation, humming a passage from a quartet. When she got out, she said it was swell, really swell, that everything was top-notch and regards to all the doctors he would ever meet and if he listened to them, he would grow up to be a better animal than old Keats, any time of the day. He couldn't tell from her voice if she was kidding or not.

He slid the car under the electronic doors, everything still working beautifully. When he was back in the house again, he sent his hand into the clothes closet in the hall, this time like a homing pigeon with a message, dropped the keys into the cashmere pocket and as he did so, he had a strange and pleasant feeling of loyalty, somehow, he felt dutiful. As he climbed the stairs to his room, he remembered himself flung against the slope of Mount Royal, the woman's face in his lap. He slipped into his bed and lay back with a smile. He had found a use for his new treasure. At last, he and his father could have something to talk and joke about together.

AFTERWORD

By Alexandra Pleshoyano, editor

When Leonard Cohen was interviewed on publication of *The Favourite Game* in 1963, he was careful to explain that the novel was not his first, implying the existence of an earlier novel, worthy of note even though unpublished. This novel, along with a collection of short stories and plays, can be found in the Leonard Cohen archive at the University of Toronto, and it is presented in this volume for the first time.

These early works are notable for several reasons. In them, we see the emergence of Leonard as a storyteller with protagonists who seem almost to be the author's alter ego, a technique that recurs in his later work. We find characters encountering and revealing inner demons in a harsh and almost brutal light, and the use of irony and humor. And throughout, the reader encounters early explorations of themes that will occupy Leonard for his entire artistic life: the sacred and profane dimensions of sexual desire; the longing for an ideal woman, capable of a liberating love; a search for freedom in a world of limitations and boundaries; the challenge—and even incapacity—to embrace commitment; feelings of alienation; the dread flowing from a sense of unworthiness coupled with an aspiration for the transcendent and the beautiful.

The manuscript is divided into three parts: Leonard's first, unpublished novel entitled A *Ballet of Lepers*; fifteen short stories; and a playscript entitled *Trade*.

The novel A *Ballet of Lepers* was written at Leonard's childhood home located on Belmont Avenue in Montreal. Some of Leonard's letters in the archive attest that it was written between 1956 and 1957. There are four drafts of this unpublished novel. Contrary to what we might expect, the second draft is the most complete version, and is the one retained here, however part of the last page of this draft has been ripped apart and is missing, so I transcribed the last page of the third draft to replace it.

In the second part of the book, the fifteen short stories are assembled according to the location where each had been written. The second part of the book starts with "Saint Jig," "O.K. Herb, O.K. Flo," and "Signals," which were all written at Leonard's childhood home. The fourth story, "Polly," was written between September 1956 and the spring of 1957 when Leonard, twenty-two years old at the time, was enrolled for some postgraduate studies at Columbia University in New York. He was living at the International House located on Riverside Drive. The fifth and sixth short stories, "A Hundred Suits from Russia" and "Ceremonies," were both written between 1957 and 1958 when Leonard was living on Mountain Street in downtown Montreal.

The seventh short story, "Mister Euemer Episodes," was written during that same period, with the archive version of it bearing a different title, "Marriage of the Virgin." The eighth short story, "The Shaving Ritual," was written in Montreal in 1958, but no specific address is mentioned. Due to the same characters—Mr. and Mrs. Euemer—being present in the seventh, eighth, and ninth short stories, I chose to place the three consecutively. An alternate draft of this story in the archive uses the title "Barbers and Lovers." Leonard mentioned that the ninth short story, "Lullaby," was written on Mountain Street and thus we can presume that stories sharing those characters could have been written at the same location between 1957 and 1958. The tenth and eleventh stories, "A Week is a Very Long Time" and "The Jukebox Heart" were also written on Mountain Street.

The twelfth short story, "David Who?" was written on the island of Hydra in Greece in 1960, and was in earlier drafts called "Diary of a Montreal Lecher." The thirteenth short story, "Short Story on Greek Island," could also have been written in 1960 in Hydra.

The fourteenth short story stands out because of its Hebrew style; Leonard wrote it without any title, capital letters, punctuation, or accents, just a few spaces in between the end of a sentence and the beginning of the other, suggesting some invisible punctuation to the reader. Following the Jewish tradition—which is how Leonard proceeded to entitle each of his fifty psalms published in *Book of Mercy*—I am using the first few words of this short story by way of title "ive had lots of pets." This short story "ive had lots of pets," as well as the fifteenth and final one, "Strange Boy with a Hammer," could have been written anytime, and anywhere, between 1956 and 1960.

The third and final part of the manuscript presents a playscript, *Trade*, written between 1957 and 1958 when Leonard lived on Mountain Street in downtown Montreal. According to an exchange of letters written in 1961, *Trade* kindled Canadian Broadcasting Corporation producer Robert Weaver's interest, but it is not clear what happened afterwards.

We know from Leonard's letters in the archive that he tried consistently to have these works published. While rejection is a part of many young writers' careers, in Leonard's case, it is some-what puzzling given the success of his early books of poems, *Let Us Compare Mythologies* (1956) and *The Spice-Box of Earth* (1961), collections that in a sense bookend the works contained in this volume. These previously unpublished works provide a unique window into the early art of Leonard Cohen.

Alexandra Pleshoyano
Ste Catherine de Hatley (Quebec)

LEONARD COHEN's artistic career began in 1956 with the publication of his first book of poetry, *Let Us Compare Mythologies*. He published two novels, *The Favourite Game* and *Beautiful Losers*, and ten books of poetry in his lifetime, including *Stranger Music: Selected Poems and Songs* and *Book of Longing*. His latest poetry collection, *The Flame*, was published posthumously in 2018. During a recording career that spanned almost fifty years, he released fourteen studio albums, the last of which, *You Want It Darker*, was released in 2016. Cohen was inducted into the Rock and Roll Hall of Fame in 2008, received a Grammy Lifetime Achievement Award in 2010, and was awarded the Prince of Asturias Award for Literature and the Glenn Gould Prize in 2011. He died on November 7, 2016.